Honor Bound

Rebecca Tran

Published by Rebecca Tran, 2020.

This is a work of fiction. Similarities to real people, places, or events are entirely coincidental.

HONOR BOUND

First edition. February 9, 2020.

ISBN: 979-8230401032

Written by Rebecca Tran.

To my loving family

Chapter 1

Hallie

Hallie sat at her desk in her small cubicle covered in sketches, magazine clippings, and post it's trying to figure out her next assignment. Normally it wasn't so hard, but she hated the subject matter. She sat back with a huff annoyed. It shouldn't be this difficult. Hallie glanced at her watch it was past six. She was off work half an hour ago.

Stretching as she stood, Hallie saw Jeff over the line of cubicles. She could barely see over them, while Jeff had several inches to spare. Both of them worked for an advertising company. Hallie was in the art and creative design department. She helped think up the ideas and went on photo shoots. Jeff was in the layout and graphic design department. He helped make the presentations and finished product. They met almost a year ago at a work function. Despite being a little work-obsessed, he absolutely adored Hallie.

Jeff kissed her cheek and asked how her day went. Hallie looked hatefully at her cluttered desk. Then she sighed and said it was fine. Hallie hated when she couldn't figure out a project. Jeff rubbed her back guessing the problem. He offered to take her to dinner. Hallie knew he wanted more and really wasn't in the mood. She told Jeff she was tired and just wanted to go home. He shrugged and said they could watch a movie. That was a compromise at least Hallie's roommate Jenny would be home. With the right signal, she'd make a pest of herself.

Hallie sat on the couch beside Jeff after devouring the Chinese food they grabbed on the way home. Jeff settled in next to her with the remote in hand. Jenny plopped down next to them still eating lo mien. She asked question after question about the movie until Jeff abandoned it completely. He stood up to go. "What time am I picking you up for the party tomorrow?"

"I'm not going, Jeff." Hallie protested.

"Party? Why wouldn't you go to a party? Jenny asked.

"It's the company's annual anniversary party. I never go. I don't fit in there." Hallie explained.

"What time does the party start?" Jenny asked.

"Eight," Jeff told Jenny.

"You're going to that party," Jenny told Hallie then looked at Jeff. "She'll be ready at 7:30."

The next evening Hallie mingled with Jeff clinging tighter to his arm with every new person. Jeff patted her hand and kept moving around the room. He talked to person after person. Each one was more important and more glamorous than the next. Hallie just wanted to throw up. She couldn't do it. Finally, she let go and slipped away. Jeff glanced at her as she did. Hallie heard his lame excuse but really didn't care.

Thankfully she found a chair near an open window and was able to get some fresh air. The wave of nausea was passing. The one to escape was not. She couldn't believe she let Jenny talk her into this. There were too many people here. They were all important and pretty. Hallie was none of those things. She always felt like a party crasher.

Hallie got to her feet. She leaned against the wall taking a deep breath preparing herself to go back in and find Jeff. She had to do this, she had to. Yet the walls felt like they were closing in on her. Hallie tried to step back but forgot there was a wall there. It sent her into a full panic attack. She was trapped.

'Breathe' Hallie told herself. The air was stuffy. 'Breathe' the air was stale. 'Breathe' the air was so hot. 'Breathe' the air smelled of summer? 'Breathe' there were hints of apples and grass. Hallie opened her eyes as a breeze ruffled her dress. She cursed out loud without meaning to.

A valley of spring green grass spread out before Hallie. A castle straight out of a storybook sat in the distance. Smaller manor houses dotted the hillsides. An orchard spread out around her. Behind her, she could see the ballroom their company rented for the party through what looked like a doorway. The breeze blew again carrying the scent of wildflowers and damp earth. The grasses and flowers swayed in the breeze. It was so beautiful there Hallie swore she was dreaming.

Faolin

It was another dull, monotonous day. Faolin sat in his room brooding again. How could he pass the time? Nothing of interest happened in Underhill in over a century. Well nothing of interest to him. His uncle arranged hunts and parties, but it was pointless. There were the occasional trips to the mortal realm for a wee bit of fun with their women. Faolin was through with mortal women though. So he had little to occupy his time.

Faolin heaved a sigh as he drummed his fingers on the arm of his chair thinking. Then he felt it. His guardian Taise, the white wolf, saw something that didn't belong in Underhill. Faolin was on his feet with sword in hand and a grin on his face. This is what he'd been waiting for. He opened a portal to the orchard and stepped through.

What Faolin found at the tree line was not what he was expecting. The intruder was a beautiful woman. She was short and curvy in a dress cut to flatter her figure. Her short auburn colored hair was cut at the jaw line bringing out high cheekbones, a slender nose, and pale blue eyes. Faolin couldn't take his eyes off her. Someone called to her. She turned, leaving Underhill. All Faolin was left with was her first name, Hallie.

Faolin's first thought was to follow her. He summoned his magic to form the gateway and stopped. Faolin was bound by honor and magic to report the intrusion to the king. He let out an oath as he formed a portal.

King Oberon was at dinner when Faolin barged in. The Taise trotted beside him. King Oberon set down his turkey leg and sat back in his chair. "And to what do we owe this pleasure?" he asked put out.

"An intruder in Underhill. A mortal woman. She shouldn't have been able to get in. Someone needs to see how she did it and stop her." Faolin explained.

"And who do you propose we should send?" King Oberon asked.

Faolin sighed as if put out. "I'll go. I have nothing better to do." Queen Titania smirked a little. She probably knew what he was up to. Faolin really didn't care as long as he was allowed to find that mortal.

Hallie

Hallie still didn't know how she let her panic attack get that bad that she imagined a fantasy world. It was so real. Jeff was annoyed by her disappearing act that he said it was time to leave. Somehow she'd sat in that chair for almost an hour. Jeff swore he looked for her there, but Hallie hadn't moved.

Jeff was normally a very patient and understanding man. When it came to his career though he was intent on getting ahead, nothing was going to stop him. Sometimes Hallie held him back, and he got irritated. Tonight was one of those times. He dropped her off and went to some after party. Tomorrow Jeff would call and apologize. Hallie sighed as she climbed into bed.

Hallie closed her eyes and was back in the valley. She saw every detail like she was there. The scent was enchanting. Hallie took in every detail, memorizing it. If she had a dream like this, she wanted to paint it. Then she heard it, a low snarl that quickly turned into a growl. Hallie turned and found herself face to face with a huge white wolf.

Not knowing what else to do Hallie ran. The wolf let her go. It wanted the hunt. She was in trouble now. It knew it could catch her. Hallie ran faster. The wolf gave chase. It didn't take long for Hallie to tire. She wasn't a runner despite her sporadic attempts to exercise. Her chest was burning, and her legs were cramping. Hallie scrunched her eyes closed and dug deep for one last burst hoping to reach a tree.

It didn't take long for Hallie to run into something. It wasn't a tree though. It was a wall of solid muscle. Strong arms held Hallie up as her legs gave out. The wolf snarled behind her and Hallie whimpered in panic. The man whistled, and the wolf sat on its haunches like a trained dog. Hallie looked up at her rescuer, but she couldn't see his face. It was her dream damn it. Why couldn't she see his face? Hallie sat up breathing hard when her alarm went off. It was morning already.

Hallie hated Mondays. Especially Mondays when she had to go to photo shoots, and photo shoots with skinny spoiled models were the worst. Today was the perfect trifecta of terrible. After the weekend that she had this was the icing on the cake. Yesterday was a wasted day. Once she woke up completely from that dream, she had to draw as much as she could. It turned into an all-day project. Even Jenny started getting worried. Combine that with the party and the weekend was just terrific. Hallie sighed as she trudged into work.

Jeff had flowers waiting on Hallie's desk when she arrived at her cubicle. That was at least one good thing that would happen today. Hallie set her things down before answering her phone that was already ringing. The senior art director wanted to make last minute changes. Halie was going to have to scramble. She grabbed her purse and rushed out the door.

Hallie watched the photo shoot with rapt attention. All her energy went into the last minute details. It was up to her to make sure this went exactly the way it was supposed to. The photographer was starting with the first model. This was going to be a long day. They had two models with two outfits each and a set change. Hallie sighed checking her watch.

One of the crew walked past carrying a crate. Normally Hallie wouldn't have cared or even noticed. This guy though was built. He was over six foot tall with the arms of Greek sculpture. Hallie could only guess what the rest of his body looked like. He had blonde hair and blue eyes in a perfectly chiseled face. It was enough to make any woman stop and stare. Hallie shook herself. She had to focus, not drool over some new crewman. She took one last look before focusing on the shoot once more.

"Maybe next time you should ask your photographer to take a picture." A voice behind Hallie said making her jump.

Hallie hadn't expected anyone to come up behind her. She faced the unknown voice and couldn't believe her eyes. It was the new crew member. It was everything Hallie could do to keep her mouth from hanging open. "Sorry," she apologized lamely.

"Don't be," he shrugged surveying the shoot. "Maybe someone should tell those women carrots are for rabbits."

Hallie laughed a little. She couldn't help it. He meant what he said. He didn't see anything wrong with it either. He had a slight accent which meant he didn't grow up in the States at least. If Hallie had to guess she'd say Ireland. "That's what sells," Hallie shrugged.

"Then you Americans are daft. I like a little meat on a woman's bones." He turned and headed off once more giving Hallie a good look.

Faolin

Faolin found the mortal easily enough. His guardian was able to help track her down. Getting hired at her work wasn't hard either. She, however, was going to be more challenging than he thought at first. He found out from the rest of the crew she already had a suitor. She also had her own residence which meant she was independent. What would she need him for?

The look she gave him though was unmistakable. She was interested. That was something in his favor at least. Most mortals found it hard to resist the Fay. Still, he had a few obstacles in his way. Now that she noticed him Faolin needed to get her attention.

One of the male models was headed towards the table of food. Faolin grinned as he waved a hand and looked away. There was a crash behind him and a lot of concerned voices. Faolin slowly got up from the table with everyone else to see what happened. The poor man tripped and fell. He couldn't put any weight on his ankle. What a shame Faolin agreed with his co-workers.

Hallie was surveying the situation and making notes. She had the injured man taken to medical help and the mess at the buffet cleaned up. She had a crew member clear the aisle. In less than five minutes everything was sorted out; everything that was except the missing model.

Hallie scanned the list in her hand and made a phone call. Then she talked to the photographer. There was another phone call, and Faolin thought she might throw her phone. Faolin struck up a conversation with the crewman beside him although he was keenly aware of where Hallie was. She marched straight up to him and tapped him on the arm.

"I need a word with you," she more demanded than asked. "please," she said as an afterthought. It wasn't what Faolin expected. He thought for sure she'd be a mousy little woman. He hated to admit it, but this was a turn on.

Faolin excused himself stepping aside to speak with Hallie, "I need you to step in for the missing model. Can you do that? All you have to do is wear the clothes smile and do what the photographer says."

"It seems really hard. I think I can handle standing there and looking pretty though." Faolin told her as he crossed his arms over his chest.

"Sorry I didn't mean it like that. I meant it's not something everyone wants to do. Some people feel silly. I hate having my picture taken." Hallie apologized.

Faolin relaxed. "Apology accepted."

"Thanks, you're a lifesaver Mr..." Hallie prompted.

Faolin had the sudden urge to tell her his real name. Why he had no idea. Names held power over the Fay and were rarely told to anyone save King Oberon and family. Why would he have the urge to give her that kind of power over him? He offered his hand instead "Liam Martin,"

"Thanks again Liam," she shook his hand. It was soft, and he couldn't help noticing how good she smelled. Hallie cleared her throat as she let go. "I'll show you what's going on." She turned away quickly. Faolin was sure she was blushing though. This may not be as hard as he thought.

Hallie

Hallie didn't know who hired the Irish Adonis that saved her shoot on Monday. She owed them a steak dinner though. Without Liam, she'd have been sunk. Jeff didn't think it that big of a deal. He'd never dealt with a modeling agency before or models. She couldn't get one at a moment's notice. The senior creative director wasn't budging either. He liked the replacement though. He was so pleased he was recommending Hallie for a small promotion.

Jeff saw Hallie's career advancement as an opportunity to progress their relationship as well. He wanted to move in together. Hallie wasn't so sure. Moving in with Jeff was a big step. She'd have to give up her place with Jenny, and she wasn't sure she was ready to do that. Hallie didn't know why he was in such a rush. They'd only been dating a year.

Thursday afternoon Jeff sat on the corner of Hallie's desk waiting to go to lunch. He told her about yet another apartment he found. Hallie let him talk. She didn't want to bring up a sensitive subject at work. She grabbed her purse as she stood up. Liam chose that exact moment to walk past with a ladder. Hallie tried not to notice. How could she not though? He was gorgeous.

Jeff asked if Hallie was even listening. She tore her eyes away focusing on Jeff once more. Hallie insisted she'd been listening to him prattle on about an apartment she didn't want to move into. Jeff stopped. He looked at her a moment a little shocked. Hallie mumbled an apology and said maybe a different one. Jeff took her hand as they walked out.

Hallie plopped into her chair after lunch. It was a disaster. She meant to talk to Jeff about not moving in together. Instead, she looked at ads for five different places. Hallie put her head down on her desk with a groan. She still felt guilty about snapping at Jeff earlier. It kept her from telling him the truth.

"If you don't want to move in with him, you should just tell him." A voice told her.

"I know," she half whined.

"You're an independent woman. There's no shame in that." The voice told her.

Hallie looked up into Liam's smiling face as he leaned on her cubicle wall. She was so embarrassed. "You heard us earlier?"

"Sorry I had to fix the light." He nodded towards the light above the two cubicles next to her. "He should understand if he cares about you."

Hallie sighed. "I know, but Jeff has this picture of where he wants to be in five years, and he wants me there with him." Hallie rubbed her temples. "He says this is the first step."

"But is it your picture, Hallie?" Liam asked.

Hallie sat up and looked at Liam. That was mistake number one. He took her breath away every time. Mistake two was actually talking about her problems with him. She didn't even know him. Why did she feel like she could tell him anything? Hallie told Liam how focused Jeff was on his career. It never bothered her. Hallie's job was just that. Sure she enjoyed it, which was a major bonus, mostly though, it paid the bills. If Hallie had her choice, she'd be a full-time artist.

Glancing at the clock, Hallie realized she'd prattled on for 15 minutes. Hallie hastily apologized. Liam shrugged. He insisted he didn't mind, it kept him from fixing a broken chair a little longer. Angela from the art department buzzed into her cubicle talking about their next project. She didn't even notice Liam until he picked up his ladder and walked down the row of makeshift offices. Angela stopped to stare then. Hallie knew how she felt.

Chapter 2

Hallie

Two weeks later Hallie sat in a meeting with her boss, a senior creative designer. Sharon was a nice woman outside of work but a real pain to work for. Everything had to be done to her exacting standards, or there was hell to pay. Now, Sharon, had her mind made up that Liam had to model in her newest campaign and he didn't want to. She knew Hallie got him to model once and gave her the task of doing it again.

Hallie sighed as she got up. She'd only seen Liam in passing the last several days. How was she going to find him now? She shut down her laptop and reached under the table for her bag. Under the left table leg was a wadded up piece of paper keeping it from wobbling. Hallie shook her head. Then she sat up. Why had she been so stupid? They worked at the same company.

Back at her desk Hallie strummed her fingers on her desk as she waited. She was nervous. Why was she nervous? Liam came down the row of cubicles, and she couldn't think about it. Hallie sat up smiling cheerily. She tried not to ogle him this time and was only partially successful. Liam pretended not to notice.

Liam leaned on her cubicle making Hallie nearly forget why she needed to speak to him. Deciding to get it out as quickly as possible, she cleared her throat and said it all in one rush. Liam stared at her a moment as he absorbed what she said.

"So this Sharon, your boss, wants me to model again and sent you to ask me?" Liam considered. "I don't know, " Liam hesitated.

"We'll pay you, of course," Hallie assured him.

"I'm not worried about that." He shook his head. "I'm supposed to keep a low profile." Hallie was confused. "It's a family thing."

"It's a small ad campaign. I'm sure it won't make it to anyone important." Hallie tempted. "I would be a huge favor for me."

"Oh, in that case, we can settle the score straight away. Have dinner with me Friday night." Liam suggested.

"Liam I have a boyfriend." Hallie protested.

Liam smiled, "That wasn't a no,"

"No," Hallie insisted.

"What's wrong Hallie?" Jeff asked making her jump.

Hallie stood up her cheeks blazing red. "Um Jeff, this is Liam. He helped out on that ad campaign." Hallie explained. Jeff thought a moment then took Liam's hand thanking him. "Sharon wants him in another ad. I was just asking him."

"And I was just refusing unless the company treated me to dinner. And Hallie would have to personally fill me in as we ate." Liam explained.

"You can do that Halle," Jeff shrugged.

"He means alone, Jeff." Hallie clarified as Liam grinned.

Jeff pulled Hallie to the side. "It's one evening Hallie, and this is what Sharon wants. Be professional and get him to do the shoot." Hallie stared at him. She couldn't believe he didn't care that she'd go out with another man. "Come on Hallie, this was a great opportunity don't blow it. I trust you."

Hallie sighed as she pulled her arm out of Jeff's grip. "When and where?" She asked Liam.

"I'll meet you at your desk after work on Friday." He smiled again.

"You are doing the shoot right?" Hallie asked.

Liam sneered, and she wondered why. “I gave my word,” He confirmed as he walked away.

Hallie looked at Jeff who shook his head. Neither of them knew what that was about.

Friday evening took forever to arrive. Hallie was nervous. She didn’t know what to expect at dinner. Was Liam asking her out on a professional level or personal? She wore a nice dress to work and slipped on the heels she brought. At least she looked nice.

Liam stopped at her desk at precisely 5:30pm. He wore khaki pants and a light blue button-up shirt. He’d changed from the jeans and plain black tee he wore earlier that day. Hallie thought he was handsome before, his sex appeal just ratcheted up several notches. She forgot to breathe for a moment. Liam said hello and offered his arm.

Hallie reluctantly took Liam’s arm. She was still so unsure what he wanted. Liam smiled though and acted like a perfect gentleman. The restaurant was only a few blocks away. It was a gorgeous evening, and Hallie never minded walking. She wasn’t so sure about his choice though. Hallie had a budget for work expenses. This place looked like it would be a whole month’s allowance. Sharon did say she wanted Liam whatever Hallie had to do though.

Liam held the door for Hallie. The food smelled amazing. However, the line at the hostess station was ridiculous. It didn’t seem to bother Liam though. He saw a waiter and waved him over. A few quiet words and they were in. Hallie couldn’t believe it. The waiter sat them at a booth in the back of the restaurant. He pulled a reserved sign off of it as he left. Hallie had to say she was impressed. When she asked about it, Liam said he used to work there. Hallie wasn’t convinced, but she let it drop.

It didn’t take long for their server to come over for their order. Hallie had no idea what to order. The entire menu was in French. Liam smiled and offered to order for her. What else could she do? An older man with greying hair and cunning eyes came out with a bottle of wine. He barely glanced at the table as he presented the bottle to Liam. When he accepted the wine though, the steward's eyes grew wide. He stared at Liam like he'd seen a ghost. Before the steward could utter a word, Liam asked him to pour the wine and leave.

Hallie never saw Liam be rude before, to anyone. Why would he treat that poor wine steward so cruelly? She couldn't understand it. Maybe Liam had worked here, and there was bad blood between the two. Whatever it was, it wasn't her concern.

Liam asked her the most random questions as they ate dinner. Most people ask where you grew up. Liam asked where her family was from and what her heritage was. He wanted to know if she had any family traditions and who she took after. The questions were a nice departure from the norm, but it was still odd.

Hallie had to admit Liam was good company. He was kind and friendly; well friendly to most. He was charming really; although she would never tell him that. Hallie reminded herself constantly that she was with Jeff and this was just business. A man like Liam would never be interested in a woman like Hallie.

Toward the end of dinner, Hallie managed to steer the conversation where she needed it to go. The photo shoot. Liam sat back in the booth sipping his wine. He picked at a crack in the wall as if bored. Finally, he faced her. He was annoyed again. Hallie wasn't going to take it. She'd done nothing wrong. She told Liam as much, and he began to laugh. He assured her that he would do the photo shoot now that she held up her end of the bargain.

Hallie breathed a sigh of relief. At least this dinner wasn't a waste. She played with the gold chain on her neck that she always wore. Her father's pendant was a reassuring sight as it swung free. Liam glanced at her and sat up straighter. Hallie had no idea why.

Faolin

Faolin was annoyed. He set up this whole dinner hoping to get some answers from Hallie. If that failed, he hoped to at least get her attention. He received neither. She was only interested in the damn photo shoot. He sat back enjoying the last of his wine as she brooded across from him. This night hadn't gone at all as he planned.

A glint of gold in the dim light caught Faolin's attention. Hallie wore a necklace he hadn't noticed before. She played with the chain now making the pendant dance. It was an odd choice for a young woman: a small grey-blue stone encircled by a small wire cage. It could be exactly what he was looking for.

"That's an interesting bauble," Faolin commented motioning to Hallie's pendant.

She let it drop to her chest. Faolin followed the stone to where it rested on her blouse. Perfectly shaped breasts moved below the cloth, and he had to tear his eyes away. "A family heirloom." She shrugged. "It was my father's. He brought it with him from Ireland and always insisted it was lucky."

"Where did he get it?" Faolin asked. He leaned forward waiting for her answer.

"From his father. I told you it was a family heirloom." Hallie shook her head.

Faolin decided not to push Hallie further. She didn't know where the stone came from. If he could get closer Faolin could tell if it was linked to Underhill in some way. The waiter brought the bill, and he paid it without looking. He was sure their employer would have purchased their meal. Faolin was trying to make an impression though. Letting the company pay for their meal wouldn't bode well towards that image.

Hallie protested of course. Faolin could tell she was relieved though. She was also interested in how he managed it, handymen didn't get paid well. Faolin ignored it hoping the curiosity would pass. He offered his arm as she got out of her seat. Hallie's rich scent washed over him again drowning out the rest of the room. It took him a moment to focus on his objective as her small hand wrapped around his forearm.

The small stone around Hallie's neck looked like any other aside from the odd color. That wasn't enough to confirm Faolin's suspicions though. He needed concrete proof. Magic was always the key to Underhill like attracted like. Faolin released a small amount of magic. It wasn't enough for anyone to notice but it showed him what he needed to know. The stone drew the magic in like a dry sponge. It confirmed it came from Underhill. It did not tell Faolin how Hallie had it or if she knew how to use it.

"Are you a dreamer Hallie?" Faolin asked hoping to get some information from her.

"I'm an artist. We're all lost in some fantasy or another." She half laughed. "Some are more real than others." She shrugged then glanced up at him. Quickly, Hallie looked away. Faolin thought that was interesting. Perhaps he wasn't misjudging the situation. "I've had dreams so vivid I thought they were real." She smiled wistfully.

"What kind of dreams?" He encouraged.

"It's silly really." Hallie laughed a little. It was a light noise almost like bells. Faolin put his hand on top of hers as they walked. "Promise you won't laugh," Hallie demanded as she stopped walking.

"Of course not," Faolin brushed a stray hair from her face.

Hallie looked away, "I had a panic attack a few weeks back. The only thing that got me through was imagining I was in this fantasy world. It was straight out of some fairytale complete with a castle." She shook her head. "It's silly really, but I swear I smelled the apples in the orchard behind me. The sun was so warm, and I heard the wind through the grass." Hallie smiled.

Faolin felt the pull of magic. The stone wanted to return to Underhill. It simply used Hallie's strong emotions as fuel. She had no idea what she'd done. "It sounds like a lovely fantasy," Faolin moved on. Hallie wasn't a threat. He could return home. He'd be happier if the stone were in his possession. That wasn't going to happen unless he forced Hallie though. For whatever reason Faolin was willing to do that.

Faolin began walking again he'd been steadily heading back towards work. "So what's your story?" Hallie asked dragging him out of his thoughts.

He wasn't sure how to answer. He didn't want to lie to her "I'm here looking for something." Faolin answered finally. "It's nothing important really."

Hallie frowned, "You've come a long way for something that's not important."

Faolin scratched his head, "The object was unimportant. The search, however, was a matter of honor." Hallie stared at him in disbelief. "And I was bored." He admitted finally.

Hallie laughed slightly bringing the sound of bells with it. "I'll never understand men,"

Faolin was relieved to see the building. Hallie was every bit as enticing as Underhill. "Can I walk you home?"

"No, thanks, I'll just catch a cab." Faolin waved a cab down for her. "Thanks, they never stop for me" She ducked inside the car but didn't close the door. "Well, goodnight then." She shut it and waved. The cab zoomed off a moment later. Faolin went into an empty alley before opening a gateway to Underhill.

Hallie

Hallie hadn't seen Faolin for three weeks. He came to the photo shoot then disappeared. Human resources had no clue what happened to him. His manager had no choice. He had to fire him. Sharon was pissed now. She owed Faolin money and was hoping to deliver it in person so she could ask him to do another shoot. Sharon couldn't do that, and somehow it was Hallie's fault.

All Hallie wanted to do at the end of another crappy week was sink into a hot bath and sip a glass of wine. It sounded simple enough as she went into the bathroom. Jenny was in the mirror with her headphones on finishing her makeup for a date. Hallie shook her head as she turned the handle for the hot water.

The pipes rattled a moment then spit out rusty water. Hallie hoped it would run clear in a minute, but it only got worse. She tried the sink with the same result. To make matters worse, the water was cold when it should have been hot. Hallie groaned in frustration. She hated dealing with the building super. Luckily he responded to texts. At least she didn't have to talk to him for a little while.

Hallie's first text explained what the problem was and she braced herself for the argument that waited. Instead, she received a very prompt response that he'd be right up. Hallie couldn't believe it. Maybe her luck finally turned.

No sooner had Jenny flew out the door than the super knocked. Hallie wished he'd have been a few minutes earlier. She hated dealing with him on her own. Squaring her shoulders, Hallie marched to the door and yanked it open. The person behind it was the last one she ever expected.

Liam waited patiently on Hallie's doorstep in jeans and a dark grey t-shirt. He held a toolbox in one hand and a phone in the other. What the hell was he doing here though? She was speechless a moment as his topaz eyes stared down at her. He seemed just ass shocked to see her.

"This apartment is leased to Jennifer Ellis," Liam said confused.

"My roommate, Jenny. What are you doing here?" Hallie asked.

Liam shifted under her stare. "The old super quit suddenly and I needed a job that came with a place to stay." He looked away from Hallie "My situation is complicated."

"Oh," Hallie stepped aside. "Come in then." Liam stepped through. Hallie couldn't help watching as he shoved his phone in his pocket. He turned suddenly facing her to confirm where the water heater was. Hallie stammered a moment before recovering. Liam didn't seem to notice. Hallie breathed a sigh of relief.

Less than an hour later, Liam, had the water heater and the pipes fixed. Hallie couldn't believe how fast he worked. She'd given up on a bath and settled for sketching on the couch with a glass of wine. She was deep in thought when Liam tapped her on the shoulder. Hallie jumped. Liam apologized smiling slightly. "You're pretty good."

Hallie set her sketch pad down as she got up. She hated when others watched her work. It was all she could do to get Liam out the door. As soon as she closed and locked it Halle cursed. She hadn't even mentioned the photo shoot Sharon wanted him to do. Briefly, she thought about going after him. It could wait now though, she knew where he lived.

Faolin

Faolin smiled as he left Hallie's apartment. He'd surprised her just as he hoped. She thought he'd left for good only to reappear in her life suddenly. They say absence makes the heart grow fonder and he hoped it would work on Hallie. In this case, he wasn't so sure. She was eager to get him out the door. That was never a good sign.

Setting his toolbox down on the table Faolin plopped into a chair. This old building would allow him plenty of opportunities to see her. Thankfully in his years of self -exile he spent a lot of time learning to fix mortal things. Although, this was going to require a lot of work. He heaved a sigh as he made a list of everything he noticed so far. Faolin shook his head, a ton of work. Tomorrow was another day and another chance to see Hallie.

The sun rose early the next day. It took little time to dress and eat breakfast. Things were so much simpler in the mortal realm. It was one of the few reasons Faolin liked it. He gathered the supplies he needed and went up the lobby. The paint here was cracked and peeling. The old super was far too lazy. Faolin would have to scrape before he could paint.

An hour into his work the building tenants began passing him on their way out. Most of them were upset, and he had no idea why. They should have been happy he was fixing the building. Faolin shrugged it off as he continued to scrape the old paint away.

Then he saw her. Hallie came down the hall in black slacks, pink and black striped shirt and pink flats. Her hair bounced as she walked. Hallie sipped her coffee absently until she reached him. Then Hallie stopped. Instead of a pleasant good morning, he received a scolding for starting work so early. Faolin protested, but Hallie didn't stick around to hear it. She marched off shoulders squared. Faolin couldn't help laughing. Hallie had no clue what she was dealing with. He wondered if it would change anything if she did.

Chapter 3

H*allie*

Hallie was looking forward to a quiet photo shoot in the park. No Jeff and no Liam. Both of them were wearing on Hallie's nerves lately. Jeff was pushing her to move in, and Liam was always popping up in her building when she least expected it. Hallie couldn't get mad though he was fixing the place up. The last super only cared about his paycheck. At least today she had the serenity of Central Park to cheer her up.

Halfway through the shoot, the photographer started complaining about people in the background. Hallie groaned she'd have to convince them to move. So much for a relaxing day. Hallie trudged over to the soccer fields. She was surprised to see grown men there. Liam was in their midst taking long strides.

Hallie watched Liam. He ran across the field in complicated plays that she didn't understand. All Hallie noticed was the way he moved among the other players almost like he was a hunter. She was sure he hadn't been watching her, but somehow he'd known exactly where she was. He didn't stop until he scored a goal though. His teammates patted his back as he jogged over.

"Hallie," He smiled in greeting. "Are you working here today?"

"Hi Liam," Hallie couldn't help returning his smile. "We're shooting directly behind you, and you keep getting in the shot. Would you guys mind moving one field over?"

"I'm sure I could convince my mates," He nodded towards the other men who were all casually glancing their way. "You'll have to promise to make it up to me."

"How?" Hallie asked suspiciously.

Liam inspected his nails. "You could dump that boyfriend," Hallie started to say something. Liam laughed. "Just coffee Hallie, I don't know anyone aside from those blokes."

"Fine, we'll discuss it later, call the office." Hallie started off.

"I'll just stop by your apartment then," Liam called after her. Hallie sighed. Why did she agree to coffee? She glanced over her shoulder at the gorgeous man behind her. Yeah, that was why. She still didn't know why he was interested in *her*. It did feel nice though, to be desired by an Irish god. Hallie giggled to herself as she reached the shoot. The model gave her a look of contempt. Hallie really didn't care.

Jenny was annoyed all week when she found out Hallie had a date with Liam. Apparently, she'd been trying to ask him out, and he wouldn't even talk to her. Hallie couldn't help it though, Liam asked her out. She pulled on a soft blue shirt and thought about it. Liam asked her out, repeatedly. He was interested in her.

Hallie felt the panic attack hit her just in time to sit down. What was she doing going out on a real date with Liam? She had a boyfriend. Hallie forced herself to breathe. She thought about the last time she had a panic attack. The smell of the apple orchard and warm breeze was so soothing. Instantly it was there again. A cool breeze blew across her skin. Everything was dark. It was night, and the moon was half full.

A couple walked hand in hand through the field ahead of her. They were both beautiful. The man was tall and muscled with angular features. The woman was slim with rounded hips and large breasts. Her dark hair fell to her waist in perfect ringlets framing a heart-shaped face. They cuddled close laughing but stopped when they saw her. Hallie said hello. They looked horrified.

Hallie heard her name. Like last time as soon as she focused on it the couple and imaginary world disappeared. Blinking a few times Liam came into focus. He helped her stand and made sure she was steady before letting go. He looked really worried. Hallie insisted that she was fine though. Finally, Liam nodded, and they left for coffee.

Faolin

Faolin could smell the magic when he reached Hallie's door. He was sure Underhill drew her in once more. There was no telling how long ago though. This could be really bad. He found the doorway open in Hallie's bedroom. Jenny wasn't home, so that was helpful. The last thing he needed was another mortal involved. It was a small miracle that the doorway concealed itself the first time Hallie called it.

Pulling her back and closing the door wasn't hard. She was groggy and out of it for a short time though. Fighting reality was common for mortals when Underhill called to them. Hallie was lucky Faolin came when he did. She roused shortly and acted normally through coffee. Faolin said nothing of the incident. Hallie seemed happy about it.

Jeff was a common topic of discussion. That was fine by Faolin. He disliked the weasely mortal man. Jeff was always trying to control Hallie for his own gain. Faolin made a few comments here and there. It was enough to make his opinion known without looking like an ass. The last thing he wanted was for Hallie to think he disliked Jeff simply because he had Hallie and Faolin didn't.

Faolin walked Hallie back to her apartment then returned to his own. He had to go to Underhill and see what damage she caused. The gateway appeared when Faolin called to Underhill. As soon as he stepped through his Taise pushed his head under his hand. A guardian always missed their master when they were gone. This was more though. Taise looked up at him expectantly. Faolin groaned. King Oberon wanted to see him.

Stepping from one place to the next was as easy as breathing here where the land was filled with magic. Another snap of his fingers and

Faolin was dressed in a black tuxedo. While fitting the dress code, it would still irritate the king who preferred older fashions. He was in the main hall of the castle now with half the court. Faolin sighed. He hated coming here.

King Oberon sat on his throne. His wheat-colored hair hung to his shoulders, and green eyes looked like leaves of the forest. His muscular body was evident even under his brocade jacket. A crown made of the points of stag horns standing on end was his only adornment. Queen Titania sat on his right in a deep blue silk with silver embroidery gown. Her silver crown looked like leaves and starbursts accented with blue sapphires. She was a stunning woman already with pale blonde hair and eyes the color of the ocean, but tonight she was more. Her power showed, and it made her that much more frightening.

All of the court watched Faolin as he approached the King and Queen. King Oberon sneered at his tuxedo and Faolin smirked. He bowed out of respect then waited to be addressed.

"Liam, the mortal your dealing with appeared in Underhill again," Oberon growled.

"I am aware of that sire. It was an accident on her part. The stone she carries wants to come home. I was trying to get it from her before I returned."

"Trying? Since when do you try to do anything Liam?" Queen Titania scoffed. "If you wanted the stone you'd have it."

"The situation requires delicacy, my queen. I must admit that is not my strong suit."

Queen Titania laughed. "No, Liam, it is not."

"She cannot be allowed to cross back and forth." King Oberon said angrily. "A mortal in our realm without permission is unacceptable. She scared a couple witless last night."

"Yes sire, I understand." Faolin turned and left the great hall. At the back of the hall, he called the gateway. Just before he stepped through, he heard his true name guarded against others' by magic. Faolin knew who it would be.

Queen Titania wrapped her arms around Faolin pulling him into a hug. She kissed his cheek. "I can't bear you gone so long. Come home quickly." She kissed his cheek then let him go. There wasn't anything he could say. Faolin walked through the gateway without a word.

Hallie

Liam asked Hallie out the next evening, and Hallie couldn't think of a good reason to refuse. Jeff should have been enough. When Liam asked though he was the furthest thing from her mind. It wasn't like her. As soon as she hung up, she felt guilty. Hallie moved to call Liam back. Jenny stopped her midway. She pointed out that Hallie and Jeff never agreed to be exclusive. He'd also been pressuring her recently to move in together. Jenny insisted Hallie needed to test the waters with someone else first to be sure that's what she wanted. It wasn't a bad idea. Hallie reluctantly put the phone down. A few dates wouldn't hurt.

That evening Liam took her to another fancy restaurant that Hallie was sure he couldn't afford. Somehow he walked past the long line of people waiting at the door to get in. They sat down in a quiet corner booth away from the crowd, and the waiter brought over menus. Liam ordered the wine and let Hallie order her own entrée.

They talked the whole evening about everything she could imagine. Hallie had no idea Liam would know so many different things. She could have listened to him for hours though. Liam wanted to know about her life as much as she wanted to know about his. He kept steering the conversation back to that. Hallie thought her life was boring though.

It was just Hallie, and her mom after her dad died when she was two in a car wreck. Her mom Jane worked as a waitress in a diner near their home in New Jersey. After school and on weekends Hallie studied in a booth at the diner until she was old enough to work part-time. Then she got a job at the same diner. Eventually, she got a full scholarship to Pratt in New York where she studied art. Holidays and summers were spent working at the diner until she graduated and found a job.

It wasn't much, but they were happy. Hallie's mom made sure she always had everything she needed too. Other kids had fancy cars or expensive trips. Hallie's education always came first. Her mom made sure that. When she wanted to study abroad one summer that there was money set aside for her to do so.

Hallie's mom never re-married either. She dated a few times. She even had a long-term boyfriend. When it came to actually getting married though, she just couldn't do it. Hallie thought part of her mom died with her dad. There was a new man recently, and Hallie hoped it would go somewhere now that Hallie was out on her own.

Liam listened to everything with rapt attention. He asked questions now and then to clarify what he didn't understand. It was great for someone to finally hear what she had to say and not try to fix everything.

Hallie tried to get the same information out of Liam, although he was pretty tight-lipped. He said his parents died when he was young. It meant his aunt and uncle raised him. They never had children of their own, so he was like their own son. Then things went south when he got into a fight with his uncle, and they haven't gotten along since. It wasn't the whole story, but it was something.

Liam walked her home after dinner. He held her hand the whole way as she leaned into him. Hallie didn't want to admit how nice it felt. He was a solid presence next to her. He didn't judge or push her for personal gain. Liam just wanted to be with her. She still hadn't figured out why, although she loved every minute.

Jeff called that evening. Of course, he wanted to know how the date went. Hallie told him it wasn't any of his business. He asked if he could come over the following evening. She wasn't in the mood to sleep with Jeff at the moment. If they were alone in the apartment, he would expect it. Hallie suggested dinner instead.

Chapter 4

F*aolin*

Fall was just around the corner, and all Faolin managed to do with Hallie was go on a date once a week. Sure they kissed and cuddled, but she was still dating Jeff. The only consolation was that Jeff seemed to have the same problem. Faolin was fairly certain the other man was intimate with Hallie before he arrived. At least he made Jeff take a step or two backward.

This wasn't enough though he needed real progress. He needed Jeff out of the picture. How he was going to accomplish that feat was a different matter though. Faolin tried every tactic he could. It was like Hallie was resistant to his charms. She seemed content to date both of them. Perhaps, if he pushed Jeff though, he would sabotage himself. Jeff was coming to Hallie's this afternoon. He smiled with the mischievous thoughts running through his head.

It wouldn't take much. Jeff was controlling and driven by his career. If he thought Hallie was going to mess with his perfect picture of life, he'd walk away. The first and easiest thing to take away was his sense of control over Hallie. It was slipping already now that she was dating Faolin. Then he could convince Jeff the Hallie would interfere with his career. Mortals were so simple.

Hallie

August was one of Hallie's favorite months at work. The photo shoots they did now would feature in the October magazines. That meant Hallie's holiday season started early and she had two of each. It also meant Sharon organized the annual Halloween party to get the season started.

It was one of the few work parties Hallie enjoyed. She'd gone with Jeff the last two years. He hated it Dressing up and being silly wasn't Jeff's style. That's why when Liam called to invite her she was ecstatic. He said Sharon insisted he come. Hallie smiled. Sharon was still trying to get Liam to model for them.

The Saturday afternoon before the party Liam called and told Hallie he was picking her up. He wouldn't say where he was taking her or why just that he hoped she didn't have plans for the day. He came to her door with her costume in hand. It was in a dark zippered bag so Hallie still had no idea what he'd picked out for her. She asked if she should take anything with her, but he merely shook his head. Hallie locked the door, and they were off.

Liam drove them into a nicer part of town and pulled into valet parking of a ritzy looking shopping plaza. Hallie was helped out of the car by the valet before Liam came to her side of the car with her costume still in hand. He headed directly for a salon. Hallie groaned inwardly, she hated salons. He pulled her right up to the counter and spoke to the girl.

"Ginger, this is Hallie. I've already told Heather how I want her hair done, she gets a facial and makeup too. This is her costume don't let her peek until it's time to dress."

"You're really not going to let me see?"

"Where's the fun in that?" He grinned and snatched a kiss "I'll be back to pick you up in time for the party." He handed off her costume to Ginger and left.

"He's cute." Ginger commented leaning over the counter to watch him leave.

"Yeah lucky for him too." Hallie grumped.

"Hallie, I'm Heather I'll take good care of you." A woman said as she came out from the back.

Hallie relaxed in the chair all afternoon thinking that perhaps being pampered at a salon wasn't so bad. One woman gave her a facial while another gave her a manicure, it wouldn't last, but it was nice not to have ink and chalk under her nails. Then they started on her hair and makeup. Her hair got pulled into some gorgeous updo that still managed to be simple. The few strands that escaped were gently curled. Her makeup was finished, and a thick antique gold chain was laid through her hair and across her brow.

Heather took her to a changing room where her costume waited and unzipped the bag. It was an emerald green dress right out of a renaissance fair. Hallie couldn't believe Liam was expecting her to wear it. But Heather looked at the dress with longing and urged Hallie to put it on. Hallie asked for some privacy and took off her salon smock.

Liam arrived at the salon promptly at six in t-shirt and jeans. Hallie wanted to smack him. "I have to wear this, and you're in jeans?"

"My costume's in the car." He said defensively.

They went through a drive-thru for a quick snack on the way and ate in the car in the parking lot. Hallie didn't want anyone to see her until Liam was dressed too. He let her drive to the party so he could change in the back seat. The thought scared Hallie to death. She didn't drive very often especially not in the city and Liam said he borrowed the car. Liam merely rolled his eyes and got into the back seat. At a red light, she watched in the rearview mirror as Liam pulled off his shirt. "Green Light Hallie." He chided her. From then on she kept her eyes on the road.

When she pulled up to the hotel, Liam got out of the back seat on the passenger side and came around to the driver's side to open her door. He was dressed in a Scottish kilt, white lace-up shirt with the sleeves rolled partially up, bracers on his forearms, and some kind of cape wrapped around him. He looked like he'd stepped off the set of Braveheart. He smiled flashing white teeth. "I have a sword too."

"So you're a Scottish warrior, and I'm what?"

"My Queen." Hallie couldn't help but blush at his compliment.

"Aren't you afraid they'll make fun of you for wearing a kilt?"

"No, I can get away with it. My sword is bigger." He was grinning again, and Hallie was blushing.

There was no need to worry though somehow the costume fit him and no one gave him grief. The men from the loading crew pat him on the back just like his teammates on the field did. The girls all batted their eyes at him. His costume choice for Hallie too was just as much a statement to everyone as it was to her. There was no mistaking the fact that they were together that night and he intended it to stay that way for quite some time. Hallie liked the thought, but she didn't like that he was marking his territory like a dog.

The party was a huge affair Sharon had decorations, music, food, and alcohol. Hallie and Liam danced for a long time, but Hallie drank some of the punch and shouldn't have it was alcoholic as well. Midnight rolled around Liam told her it was time to go. Hallie insisted on another drink, but he adamantly refused and carried her out. Hallie was pissed the whole way home, but Liam turned on the radio and rolled down the window. By the time they reached the apartment, she felt better. He parked the car and walked her to her door.

Jenny was still at her boyfriend's and would probably be there until early that morning. Hallie apologized to Liam and asked him to come in. He hesitated a moment then followed Hallie inside. He went right to the fridge and got a bottle of water for Hallie. She rolled her eyes but drank some just the same. She sat down on the couch, and he sat beside her.

"Liam, what gave you this idea?"

"It's part of my family history." He shrugged.

"I like it." Hallie reached up and ran her fingers through his hair then kissed him. He kissed her back pulling her closer.

His eyes shot open when she ran a hand under his kilt and up most of his thigh. "Hallie,"

"I just wanted to see if you were wearing shorts." She teased.

"I think I should go."

"But why?"

"Hallie I want us to be together. Just us, not you and me and you and Jeff. Besides, you're still buzzed. I'm not going to take advantage of you. We'll talk about this in the morning." He left Hallie alone in her room.

Hallie lay awake most of the night thinking. She hated the idea of deciding between Jeff and Liam. Mainly because one was the safe choice and the other wasn't. Liam was almost too good to be true, and that scared Hallie. What if he broke her heart, what if he left, what if he didn't. It was too much to think about. Yet the choice was easy when it came down to it.

Hallie called Jeff the next morning. She put it as gently as she could that she was picking Liam. She felt horrible, but she really didn't want to string him along. Jeff was quiet like he'd seen it coming. He merely thanked her for the honesty and hung up.

Shortly before lunch, Liam knocked on Hallie's door looking a little upset. Hallie let him in and offered him a seat. He paced instead. "Hallie you know I care for you, but this isn't fair. I can't ask this of you."

"What Liam?" he continued to pace in silence "Liam, I broke up with Jeff this morning. Now, what can't you ask of me?"

He stopped pacing and sat down "I wanted so bad to ask you to do so last night, but it wasn't right. I was going to break it off with you."

"Well, I'm glad I stopped you." Hallie smiled, he was too good to be true. She kissed him, and he gave in as he did the night before.

"Gross, I don't want to see that first thing in the morning," Jenny complained as she came out of her room.

Faolin

There was a small sense of triumph at knowing Hallie chose him. He needed more though, he needed her. The wait was starting to wear on him. Now that Jeff was out of the picture he hoped Hallie was willing to move forward. There was one way to find out and Faolin intended to try.

Friday evening Faolin took Hallie out for dinner. She was happy to see him after a long week at work. She appreciated the flowers he brought as well. Most women did whether they were mortal or Fae. He listened as she talked about work. Sharon was pressuring her again to get him to be in their pictures. He understood the woman's obsession. King Oberon would kill him though if he continued to risk exposure.

After dinner, they went for a walk in the park. It was the perfect night. The air was cool. The moon was almost full. Hallie cuddled in close. It sent warmth through his body. It had been a long time since a woman did that to him.

Faolin stopped walking and pulled Hallie close. She wrapped her arms around him staring up into his eyes. He felt like he could drown in the depths of those blue pools. Mercifully she closed her eyes as he bent to kiss her. With Hallie, it was always warm and tender. Affection radiated from her. Tonight there was more. Desire was there as well. She pulled him closer, and he deepened their kiss. His tongue explored the recesses of her mouth. Suddenly Hallie tore herself away with a slight laugh.

"Maybe we should go somewhere more private," Hallie suggested.

That was fine by Faolin. He resisted creating a portal and walked with her tucked into his arm the whole way back. She played with his fingers kissing the tips now and then. It was enough to remind Faolin she wanted him. By the time they reached his apartment his pants were uncomfortably tight from Hallie's teasing.

As soon as Faolin closed the door, he pinned Hallie to the wall with his body. His mouth covered hers and he felt the tension in her body rise. She wanted this as badly as he did. Hallie's tongue slid into his mouth before she withdrew and bit his lip slightly. The lass was intent to drive him mad with desire. One of her small hands found its way under his shirt and ran over the muscles of his chest and abdomen. Hallie smiled against his lips. Faolin grabbed her ass and pulled her closer.

Hallie giggled slightly at Faolin's forcefulness. It was the wrong move. The sound spurred his actions. If she liked that he could do so much more. Faolin picked her up and carried her to the bedroom. He tossed her on the bed then pulled off his shirt. Hallie lay back watching. She smiled with appreciation. Then he took off his pants, and she sat up a little. Faolin grinned. If that got her attention, he couldn't wait to see what she did next.

Faolin dropped his boxer briefs and stepped out of them. Hallie was on her knees on the bed staring up at him again. Damn those eyes. Faolin could lose himself in them forever. He kissed her a long moment enjoying her lips before moving down to her jaw line then her neck. Hallie moaned a little. Faolin found the edge of her shirt and took it off for her.

Hallie pulled Faolin close kissing his chest, then down his abdomen. Each spot her lips touched lit him on fire. Then Hallie sat on the edge of the bed. Faolin was confused, that is until Hallie leaned forward and took his cock in her mouth. It was an unexpected surprise that made Faolin nearly lose control at the first touch. Her tongue ran up one side and back down the other. It made Faolin gasp with pleasure. Hallie smiled at him pleased. Her left hand gently massaged his balls. Liam's only thought was how stupid Jeff was not to fight harder for her. Then her tongue flicked the tip of his shaft, and all thought left completely.

Hallie

Hallie loved pleasuring Liam. His shaft in her hand was warm and hard. It responded to her touch and made Liam moan in delight. She could do that all night just to see him happy. It wasn't what he had in mind though. Liam enjoyed Hallie's talents until he was nearly overwhelmed then he told her to lay back.

Liam unclasped her bra. Hallie slid out of it, eager to shed the extra layer. His lips found her nipple giving it a gentle tug before he sucked on her breast gently. Hallie sighed in appreciation as Liam's hands moved down her body. Every touch was an aphrodisiac. Liam removed her skirt and panties in one motion. It made Hallie laugh a little. Liam growled as he licked her inner thigh. He obviously didn't think her response appropriate.

Liam took both Hallie's thighs and placed them over his shoulders. The first touch of his tongue to her core made her jump in anticipation. The second was one long stroke that pulled her off the bed with it. The third focused on her nub and didn't let up until she was ready to scream from the attention. Anything more at the point would make her tumble into ecstasy. Liam ran his thumb over her nub circling it gently before his tongue found its way inside her. The sudden heat and pressure was more than she could bear. Hallie cried out as the first wave of pleasure took her.

Liam was smiling down at her waiting for permission to continue. Hallie's brain was fuzzy at the moment. She wasn't sure how many times she said yes. Liam pulled her into a kiss as he pushed inside her. He was bigger than she was used to and Hallie gasped involuntarily. Liam was worried he hurt her. She promised him that wasn't the case. The small break was enough to let her body adjust though.

Hallie moved first. Liam grinned that cocky boyish grin. Then he picked Hallie up. The new angle sent shivers through Hallie with every movement. Hallie had no idea sex could be this way. Her next orgasm was building already. Another few strokes and she would tip once more. Hallie cried out as the wave swept over her once more.

When she began to move Liam sat on the bed. Hallie wasn't sure why at first. Then she realized it was another new angle that felt amazing. All Jeff ever wanted was missionary. Liam, for the most part, sat back letting Hallie do as she wanted only guiding here and there. She saw the changes in his expression when she did things Liam liked.

Hallie focused on those. In a short time, she had him panting as hard as she was. She was near coming again but so was Liam. Hallie did everything she could to bring him pleasure. She switched angles slightly at the end and Hallie's whole body spasmed with her orgasm. Liam came too, lost in her euphoria.

Afterward, they both lay on the bed catching their breath. Halie smiled at Liam. She couldn't remember the last time she had sex that incredible or if she ever had. Liam, on the other hand, smiled adoringly at her a moment before getting up. He went into the bathroom with his underwear and came out a few minutes later partially dressed. The cocky grin was back. Hallie wasn't sure what to think, something was bothering him. Hallie went home that night confused.

Faolin

Faolin felt his heart warm as soon as Hallie lay breathless in his arms. He would have done anything she'd asked at that moment. The desire was there once more to tell Hallie his true name. If he did Hallie really could make him do any number of things. He never told a mortal his true name. He hadn't had the desire to either not since *she* died.

Thoughts of *her* urged Faolin out of bed and brought him back to reality. He wouldn't make the same mistake twice. He wouldn't commit himself to a mortal so easily. Yet seeing Hallie there in his bed it was hard to deny his feelings. That was the woman he'd left Underhill for. Now she was his for the taking, and he hesitated.

Hallie left as soon as she was decent. It made Faolin feel like an ass. He'd have to make it up to her a different night. First, he had to figure out what he wanted. He couldn't do that here in the mortal realm. Faolin needed Taise, and his guardian was in Under hill. He called the gateway, then stepped through to home.

Taise was always happy to see him. The white wolf circled his legs eagerly sensing Faolin's need for closeness. It calmed his thoughts, bringing clarity. Faolin wasn't sure he liked everything he found in that stillness though. There was a good reason he'd been alone for five centuries.

Faolin poured himself a drink then sat in his favorite chair. So much time had passed, yet sadness still threatened to swallow him from time to time. Taise put his head on Faolin's lap. His guardian always had the same message. 'Just breathe,' Faolin knew it all too well. He drank his wine down and took a few deep breaths until the sadness was manageable once more.

Taise caught the fleeting image of Hallie in Faolin's thoughts. The guardian perked up. He knew her face from their encounter in Underhill. His tail wagged slightly. Faolin grumbled. Of course, the beastie would like Hallie. They were both conspiring against him.

Faolin didn't really have to think about what he wanted, his heart already knew. He followed Hallie to the mortal realm for a reason. He was only faltering now because he was scared. Taise lifted his head studying Faolin. He gave the wolf a scratch behind the ear. Then got out of his chair. He had to make things right with Hallie. Faolin made an ass out of himself now he had to go beg her forgiveness. He sighed as he formed the portal and stepped through.

Faolin knocked on Hallie's door. It was still early in the mortal realm. He hoped she was awake. Her roommate Jenny answered. She shook her head and said Hallie was mad at him. Faolin showed her the flowers and theatre tickets he bought. Jenny softened. She opened the door wider letting him in.

Hallie was in her room just getting up. She looked beautiful all mussed from sleep. He sat on the bed beside her. She looked at him irritated and told him to go away. Faolin handed her the flowers and tickets. "I'm sorry Hallie, I behaved poorly last night. I was hurt in the past and worried that it would happen again. I pulled away, and I shouldn't have."

Hallie threw her arms around him, "Liam, I would never hurt you." She kissed him gently showing him that he was forgiven.

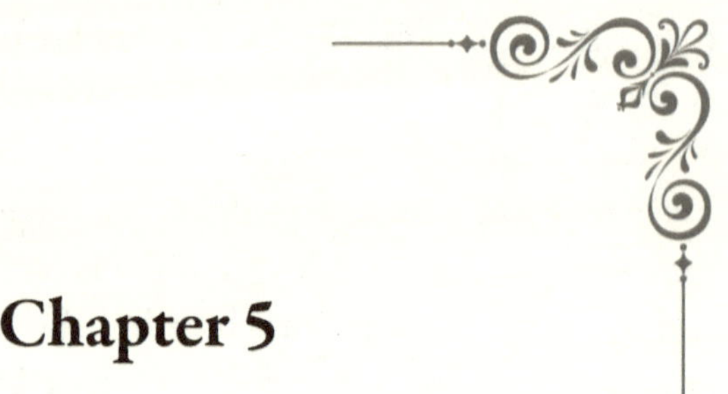

Chapter 5

Hallie

Hallie thought she must be crazy for agreeing to meet Liam's family so early in their relationship. They'd only been dating two months when Liam told her he had to see them for a bit. Of course, he waited until she was snuggled in his arms after another intense session of lovemaking. Liam could ask just about anything of her at that time. Hallie sighed. She was hopeless. Liam was too good to be true and she felt it the most when she laid in his arms like that. What did she ever do to deserve him?

Liam left for the UK nearly three weeks ago. Now Hallie was lost after getting through customs at the airport in London. She was just looking for someone not rushing around to give her directions to the train station when she saw a man holding a sign with her name on it. He was dressed in a black suit and tie. She could only guess that he was some sort of driver. When she introduced herself, he said that he had her train ticket and would take her to the station. All they were waiting on were her bags. Hallie told him the carousel number, and they marched off through the airport.

Hallie slept on the train ride. The man next to her was nice enough to wake her at her stop. He even helped her with her bag. Hallie thanked him profusely. He only smiled. She stepped off the train and saw nothing, but Liam. As soon as he saw her, he rushed down the platform to meet her. He pulled her into a heated kiss then let her go saying he missed her. He took her bag in hand and her hand in the other. Hallie couldn't help, but notice he was dressed a little nicer than normal. He wore an off-white long sleeve sweater, with a black sports coat over the top and dark jeans. Hallie was glad that she'd dressed nicely even though she'd spent all day traveling.

They climbed into a black Landrover, and Liam drove them far into the countryside. It was well past dark when they pulled up to an old manor house that was reminiscent of a castle. "My uncle's retreat." Was all Liam said as he got out. He opened the door for Hallie, but let a servant get her bags. Hallie groaned. She should have guessed by the size of the house he had servants.

He took her hand and led her inside. "Maybe I should freshen up first," Hallie suggested.

"I had a feeling you'd say that there is a dress on your bed. The third door, top of the stairs. Just follow Marvin."

Hallie closed the door to her room and looked around. There was a four-poster bed with pink and gold covers. A lounge chair that matched, an ornately carved armoire waiting for her clothes and a marble dressing table. A door on the far side led into a private bathroom. The dress on the bed was burgundy silk with a scoop neck and long sleeves. There were shoes at the foot of the bed that matched perfectly.

Hallie came downstairs 15 minutes later refreshed and wearing the dress Liam bought for her. He waited at the foot of the stairs, but his uncle was still absent. She took his hand as he whispered how beautiful she looked.

"Is it too late to go home? I'm so nervous."

"He'll love you because I do," Liam told her.

Hallie stopped it was the first time he said he loved her. "You love me?"

"Of course I do."

"I love you too." He kissed her, and all her nerves disappeared.

A gentle clearing of the throat pulled them both out of the moment. Liam let Hallie go and took her hand instead. "This must be your Hallie."

Hallie was riveted by the man who stood before her. He was tall with a broad chest, his face was more angular, and his hair looked like dried wheat. His eyes were deep forest green. He was handsome, but he looked nothing like Liam.

"My but she is pretty. Quite a vision I must say." A woman spoke, and Hallie turned. She was more beautiful than any model that Hallie ever saw, with her long limbs and perfect curves. Her hair was honey colored like Liam's, but her eyes gave away their relationship. Hallie would have guessed mother before aunt, but she looked too young.

"Hallie this is my uncle Ron and my aunt Anya."

"Pleased to meet you." Hallie offered her hand. His uncle kissed it lightly as Liam had done at their first meeting.

"Charmed" was all Anya would say. Hallie let her hand fall. "Dinner is waiting." She turned and slinked out of the room. Her black dress was backless to the waist.

Hallie leaned in close to Liam as they walked "Your aunt hates me."

"No she wants me to be happy and until she's sure you'll make me happy she's undecided."

"She's your family, not your uncle."

"My mother's sister. But my uncle and I were very close at one point in time." Hallie nodded not asking what had caused the rift.

Faolin

Faolin gave Hallie her own room while she was visiting his Uncle's home. He didn't want to presume too much. It wasn't surprising though when she slipped into his room after the house quieted down. Hallie always had a way of lighting his fire. After months apart though her touch was like an inferno. He hated having to return to Underhill even for that short amount of time. Being away from her was torture.

All of Faolin's attention was focused on Hallie that night. He lavished every affection on her. Faolin brought her to the brink of ecstasy over and over before they both tumbled over the edge together. Hallie lay in his arms afterward content and beautiful. Faolin brushed the stray hairs from her cheek enjoying the fleeting moment.

With a slight growl of frustration, Faolin eased out of bed. He pulled on his pants and went downstairs. His aunt and uncle would still be awake. He found them in the library by the fire enjoying a glass of wine. His aunt studied him a moment, however, it was his uncle who spoke.

"I'm glad to hear the mortal pleases you." His uncle smiled half laughing.

Faolin knew it meant they heard at least part of their lovemaking. At the moment he didn't care. "She pleases me more than any woman has in centuries, uncle."

His uncle stopped smiling, and his aunt set down her wine. "Can it be true?" his aunt asked studying him.

"Faolin I forbid..." His uncle started.

"Don't, I beg you. When is the last time I asked anything of you?" Faolin asked his uncle.

His uncle snarled, "At least 300 years." He let out a heavy breath. "It's too soon Faolin."

"At least grant me permission to pursue it." Faolin offered his hand.

"You know the rules." His uncle warned.

"Better than anyone" his aunt volunteered.

His uncle took Faolin's hand "Agreed. I Faolin of Underhill swear that I will abide by the rules while pursuing Hallie O'Neil."

"Honor and Magic bind thee." His uncle said formally.

Faolin felt the magic sweep over him. There was no going back now.

Hallie

Hallie watched Liam all morning for some sign, anything that would show her if there was a problem. Liam was happy though. He looked more alive if that was possible. She wasn't sure what was going on or why. Part of her wanted to know, part of her still feared she'd wake up from this dream. When Liam suggested they go horseback riding Hallie actually pinched herself. It hurt, and she assumed she was awake.

Liam helped her onto the horse and showed her how to use the reins. Hallie went slowly. She was too afraid of falling off to go any faster than a walk. Liam rode beside her patiently guiding and encouraging her. It was too much Hallie kept waiting for the other shoe to drop.

"Where did you go last night?" Hallie blurted out.

Liam stopped, and Hallie's horse stopped too. He stared at her moment. "I went to speak to my aunt and uncle. What's this about Hallie? You've been acting odd all morning."

"It's nothing Liam," Hallie swore. He stared at her and Hallie couldn't take it. He was irresistible. "I don't deserve this Liam, the vacation, the mansion, the clothes, you."

"You deserve everything I have to give and more Hallie. You brought me back to life." Liam reached across the divide and pulled Hallie close. He kissed her until her heart raced and her breath was ragged. Finally, Liam pulled away smiling. "I told you I love you, Hallie. I will do everything it takes to prove it to you." Hallie nodded still stunned by their kiss. Liam laughed a little as he kicked his horse to a walk.

His aunt and uncle came riding through the field a short while later at a breakneck pace. They stopped when they saw them, and his aunt requested to be alone with Hallie. Those piercing blue eyes stared into Hallie's. She couldn't speak, she couldn't refuse either. Liam and his uncle took off on their horses just as reckless as his aunt and uncle had been.

"My nephew cares a great deal about you." Hallie nodded. "This is not an easy thing for him."

"I love him."

"Good I hope you always remember that this will not be easy. Things never are for him." Hallie looked around the grounds here and thought of his life of ease at school. She couldn't imagine things being hard for Liam. "His uncle and I have granted him time off to do as he pleases, but he will have to return home soon. You will have to choose if you want to be with him or the others you love."

"But..."

"You will understand soon enough. My husband and I must return to our duties and will be leaving tonight I hope you enjoy our retreat."

"Thank you," they rode in silence back to the barn.

Hallie and Liam spent the rest of the week as tourists. He took her shopping and to the nicest restaurants. They found tourist traps to get lost in and historical sites to explore. The day before they were to leave they took the train into London and saw a few sites there. Liam rented them a lavish room and they made love in the huge bed the whole night. Hallie never felt more spoiled.

Faolin

Faolin didn't wait long after returning to New York to ask Hallie to move in with him. She wasn't convinced at first. Hallie was quite the pessimist. She was perpetually worried that Faolin was going to dump her. It took Jenny and him to persuade her. Once the idea settled in though, she seemed rather excited.

Living with a woman in the 15th century was one thing. They had their cookware gowns, and herbal remedies, but modern women were a whole other realm. Hallie had boxes of clothes and shoes. Another box was labeled bathroom while another was labeled towels. How many things did one woman need in the bathroom? Then came the kitchen items. Faolin didn't even want to know what Hallie brought with her. She seemed shocked at how bare his cupboards were though. Hallie made an offhand comment as she started unpacking a box.

Faolin shrugged. He went into the bedroom and found the bed piled over with clothes waiting to be hung. Faolin didn't even have a place to relax. At the moment he longed to run his fingers through Taise's fur. He missed that small comfort. For now, Hallie would have to be enough. Faolin started hanging the clothes up in the closet for her.

That night when Hallie lay snuggled in his arms, Faolin kissed the top of her head. She smiled up at him with a tender 'I love you.' It made the headaches of the day worthwhile. She fell asleep shortly afterward. He held her closer enjoying every moment. Faolin waited so long for a woman like Hallie. Now that he found her he was never letting her go.

A week after they moved in together Hallie insisted they drive to New Jersey. It was Thanksgiving, and her mother invited them to spend it with her. Faolin had no idea what to expect he never had to meet a woman's parents before. He didn't understand this holiday either. Faolin hated the unknown, yet he kept venturing into it for Hallie.

Farrah O'Neil lived in a small wooden house outside the city limits. The yard was tidy, and flowers surrounded the tree out front. The house was well kept aside from needing a fresh coat of paint. When Hallie stepped on the porch a board squeaked making her smile.

"I'm home," Hallie said cheerily, "Come in and meet my mom. She's going to love you."

Faolin wasn't so sure. Hallie really was leading a wolf to the lambs. Her mother was in the kitchen humming as she cooked. She was a slender woman with slim hips and small chest. Her hair was lighter, and her eyes were a cool grey. Aside from the structure of her face she and Hallie looked nothing alike. Then Farrah smiled. He felt her warmth. That's where Hallie got it from. Farrah O'Neil was magnetic just like her daughter. Faolin was suddenly grateful that they came. A weekend surrounded by two balls of warmth would chase away any homesickness.

Hallie's mother wiped her hands on her apron. She smiled warmly "You must be Liam, I've heard a lot about you. Hadleigh you never said he was so tall and handsome."

Faolin swore he heard Farrah call Hallie by a different name but Hallie brushed right past it. "Mom, stop, I told you what he looked like. I even sent you a picture."

Her mother laughed, "You can't be so serious all the time Hadleigh."

"Mom, Hallie, please you know I hate Hadleigh." She argued.

"I gave birth to you, and I named you." Her mother argued then looked at Faolin. "Which do you prefer?"

"I learned a long time ago not to get between mother and daughter." Faolin backed out.

Farrah smiled, "Smart man, your father would have liked him. Can you cook Liam?" Farrah handed him a knife and pointed him to a pile of vegetables.

That evening after dinner Faolin snuggled on the couch with Hallie. He wanted to ask about her name but almost dreaded it. Names were a powerful tool for the Fae. Knowing a mortal's full name gave them the ability to cast spells and manipulate them. Faolin would never harm Hallie. He wanted to know who she really was. For the Fae names told all.

Faolin kissed her neck, and she snuggled into it. "Why didn't you ever tell me your name was Hadleigh?"

"Because I hate it. I was hoping you never found out." Hallie laughed a little.

He kissed the side of her jaw. "I like it, I love everything about you. Besides the rest of your life is a long time to hide your real name."

Hallie sat up straighter. "The rest of my life?"

"I'm never letting you go, Hallie. I told you, I love you." Faolin kissed her neck then her lips. She relaxed again.

"You'll run away when you hear the whole train wreck my parents named me." Hallie teased.

Faolin shook his head and smiled, "Try me."

"Hadleigh Aoife O'Neil, my father was Irish. He came here when he was a kid and never wanted to lose his roots. My mom is mostly English and named me after her nana."

"It's beautiful, like you."

"What about you Liam Martin?" Hallie half teased.

Faolin shrugged. The urge to tell her everything returned. This time his vow held him back. Magic and honor prevented him from saying anything. "Just a name they favored." That much was true his father heard one of the mortals call another by the name Liam and like the sound of it. Fae never received true names that way though. Faolin earned his when Taise became his guardian. It was always a mystery that more of his people didn't guess his true name. Then again he received his later in life than most.

"Are you alright, Liam?" Hallie asked.

"Just lost in a memory, sorry."

Hallie

Hallie wondered where Liam went when he got that far off look in his eyes. He was too young to look so haunted. What could he possibly have seen? Liam was a mystery to her. As much as she loved him, he never talked about his past. All she knew about him was his parents died, and he was raised by his aunt and uncle. He lived and worked like anyone just trying to get by yet he came from money. Hallie asked questions here and there. All Liam would say though was that he and his uncle got into a fight. It seemed to be the root of most of things with Liam.

Eventually, Hallie let it drop. Liam would tell her when he was ready. For now, she enjoyed whatever he would give her. Right now that was Thanksgiving with her mom. They always made too much food then ate it for a week afterward. Liam never asked why. He was the perfect gentleman as he cooked beside them all morning.

That evening when they crawled into bed Hallie kissed Liam. Then she held him close for a long time. "I love you, thanks for a wonderful day."

Liam smiled warmly, "I told you I would do anything for you. This was easy. Your mother is a lovely woman. You don't look much like her though."

"I look like my father," Hallie assured him. She reached across him for the picture on the nightstand. Her father held her in his arms on the beach smiling broadly for the camera. Hallie had his eyes, his smile, his hair, and even his dimples. Only the shape of her face was her mother. Her reflection was a constant reminder of him. "He died when I was seven in a car crash. I remember he used to sing to me. It was usually songs from the radio." Hallie smiled at Liam. "Mom said he wanted me to have this." Hallie held out her pendant. It's not the prettiest thing to look at, but it was his." Hallie looked at Liam suddenly sad.

"I'm sorry Hallie," Liam kissed her gently.

Hallie drifted off to sleep in Liam's arms that night. She dreamed the most pleasant dreams. Although Hallie didn't quite remember them when she woke the next morning they reminded her of the fantasies she had during her panic attacks. There was a beautiful castle, an orchard, and a huge white wolf. The wolf should have scared her, she felt safe with it though, protected almost. When she told Liam the following morning, he didn't think it odd at all.

Faolin

Hallie was extremely busy all of December and into January preparing ads for the new year and spring. Liam worried about her constantly. He made sure dinner was always waiting for Hallie. When she was worn out he drew her a bath. When Hallie fell asleep on the couch, Liam carried her to bed. He never complained and refused to get frustrated. This was a minuscule amount of time compared to what was waiting for them. All he had to was wait a little longer.

By the time February rolled around Hallie was exhausted. When she accepted her promotion, Hallie never realized it would mean so much work. She constantly apologized to Liam, and he repeatedly told her not to worry about it. One evening Liam had dinner waiting on Hallie as normal. When she sat down though he handed her an envelope. Curious, Hallie opened it. Inside were plane tickets and a brochure for a cruise. Hallie looked up at Liam.

They left in two days. Liam already made arrangements with her boss Sharon for the time off as well. The only thing he didn't do was pack. Hallie jumped into his arms. She told him no one had ever done anything like that for her before. Liam smiled at her laughing slightly. He was always happiest when she was happy. Hallie decided to skip dinner that night. She took his hand and led them to bed.

Hallie

They found their room on the boat easily enough. It was small but had a window and its own bathroom. Liam watched as Hallie unpacked their bags. As soon as she'd put away the last sock, he pulled her down onto the bed. They missed dinner that night, but Hallie didn't care there would be snacks served later.

The next morning Hallie opened the curtain revealing crystal blue water the same as Liam's eyes. She put her bikini on ready for some sun. Liam woke and looked confused.

"In your bikini already? Where's mine." She tossed him a pair of trunks. He held them up before slipping them on. He got out of bed turning this way and that inspecting. "Why is yours so sexy and mine are well..." he shrugged. Hallie pulled out a speedo and showed it to him.

"There's your alternative." Hallie teased a little.

"These are fine." Liam relented.

"I don't know I like the speedos." Hallie slipped her arms around him moving in close. He fell back on the bed. Hallie moved in close again running a hand up his thigh "You could wear them for me later." He laughed as he kissed her. "Come on I'm starving." She got up.

"Just wait a few minutes." It was Hallie's turn to laugh.

After breakfast, Hallie went out to the pool. Before stretching out on a lounge chair, she rubbed on sunscreen and asked Faolin to put it on her back. He obliged happily, but when Hallie tried to do the same for him, he protested. Finally, Hallie just rubbed it on him. When she laid back, he did too. When she got too hot, she jumped in the pool. As she climbed out, she noticed two gorgeous women standing beside Faolin.

Hallie got out and sauntered over making it a point not to hurry. The woman with a glorious mane of auburn hair turned first even though her back had been toward Hallie. Her face was strong yet sensual with grey eyes. The second woman had red hair and blue eyes. She was pretty as well but paled beside the first woman.

"She's fair." The first woman said turning back to him.

"At least we know why you're here." The second added.

"Alainya, Oraine this is Hallie," Faolin said simply.

"We'll see you around the ship Liam, Hallie." Alainya waved as she moved off leaving Talia to follow.

Hallie watched them leave before sitting down again. "Friends of yours?"

"They think so," Liam shrugged.

The next morning they took the boat to the island. They spent all morning exploring the shops and restaurants. The afternoon was spent on the beach. It was relaxing, and Hallie loved the sun. That night as they waited for the other couple they usually ate dinner with Hallie saw the one person she never expected. Alainya slinked over to their table in her usual red. She sat down at an empty chair before Hallie could protest.

"What do you want Alainya?" Faolin asked already on edge.

"Just to say hello and see how you're enjoying your trip."

"Why are you here?" Hallie said pointedly.

"I'm just checking in on an old friend. Liam and I have history." She touched Liam's arm, and he pulled away.

Liam frowned at her "Leave us Alainya, there is nothing for you here."

"You lost the authority to command me long ago Liam." She mocked. "But I do so love these games." She got up with a Cheshire grin. Hallie wanted to wring her neck.

"What's her problem?" Hallie sneered as Alainya sauntered away.

"She's just trying to get under your skin, and you're letting her." He commented placing a hand on hers to calm her.

Over the next few days, they continued to explore whatever ports the boat stopped at. It was just the sort of vacation Hallie always dreamed of, but never thought she'd be able to afford. When they were on board, Hallie saw little of Oraine. She seemed to give them their privacy. It was only Alainya that Hallie noticed from time to time. She was always headed in the opposite direction. Hallie tried not to think Oraine was doing it on purpose to annoy her, but it seemed too frequent to be otherwise. She dared not mention it to Liam fearing he'd only say to let it go anyway.

The last night on the ship Liam asked Hallie if he could blindfold her. Hallie wasn't sure, but he insisted he wanted to surprise her. It was obvious that whatever Liam was planning was important to him and Hallie finally relented. Before covering her eyes, he pulled a picnic basket from the closet with a blanket folded neatly on top. Taking Hallie's hand, they left their room.

Liam led them through the ship for what felt like forever. Hallie had no idea where they were going except that there were lots of stairs. When they stopped, and Liam removed the blindfold Hallie found herself on the top deck that was usually reserved for elite passengers only. No one else was there. The lights were off leaving them under a canopy of stars and moonlight. Liam spread out the blanket offering her a seat. Hallie accepted as he pulled out a bottle of fine red wine. He uncorked it pouring each of them a glass before settling in beside her.

"Hallie I never say it, but I love you."

"I know you do." Hallie took a sip of wine looking at the stars.

Liam took her free hand in his kissing it gently "I know I've told you that I want you forever but I never asked before Hallie,"

"Asked what Liam?" Hallie looked back to him to see an open velvet box with a diamond engagement ring inside. The center stone was probably near two carats, and a round sapphire sat to either side.

"Will you marry me, Hallie? We'll move on your time frame, just say yes Hallie."

She smiled finally "You didn't really think I'd say no, did you? Of course, I'll marry you. I love you, Liam." He pulled her into a passionate kiss before slipping the ring on her finger. Hallie wanted a little more, but he insisted on eating first. Apparently, he'd bribed their porter into making their basket and didn't want to waste it. They would celebrate the rest of the night in their room.

Hallie got the first good look at her ring the following morning and nearly choked. She could buy a car with that amount of money, but oh how it sparkled. She got up to pack, and Liam actually got up to help. He smiled when he noticed her staring at the ring every so often. Liam wrapped his arms around her kissing her neck. He told her again how much he loved her.

Faolin

Faolin was ecstatic that Hallie agreed to marry him. He took a few days to enjoy that simple pleasure and reveled in the idea of their life together. They saw her mother the weekend after their cruise and Farrah was overjoyed as well. She wanted nothing more than to see her daughter happy and it was Faolin that did that. Mother and daughter sat down at the kitchen table and started shopping for dresses online. Faolin watched them amused. He could enjoy this one more day.

Sunday evening when they returned to the apartment Faolin knew his troubles were just beginning. He couldn't marry Hallie without telling her what he was. King Oberon wouldn't allow a mortal in Underhill without meeting her first either. Faolin needed someone to guide Hallie through the process, someone he could trust. Sadly, Faolin's options were limited.

After Hallie settled into sleep, Faolins slipped out of bed. A simple spell sent Hallie deeper to sleep assuring he had privacy. He went into the living room shutting the door behind him. Then Faolin summoned the one Fae he knew would still help him.

"Kieran, I summon thee," Faolin said plainly.

A portal appeared, and Kieran stepped through with a frown. "Liam, it's been a while."

"I require your assistance," Liam told him.

"You usually do. It's been that way since we were lads."

Liam folded his arms over his chest "I seem to remember it the other way 'round."

"What is it you want Liam?" Kieran shifted.

"If you do this properly it will clear our debt," Liam explained. Kieran looked up surprised. "Come, I will explain."

Chapter 6

Hallie

Hallie couldn't believe Liam had to work so late. Apartment 2C called a half an hour ago just as he stepped out of the shower to tell him their heater busted. It was going to take him most of the night to take it apart and fix it. The repair couldn't wait either it was 30 degrees outside.

Hallie lay in bed that night and had that feeling she was being watched. It was similar to the way she felt in her wolf dreams but not entirely the same. Something now was asking her to wake. Slowly she opened her eyes to the dark room and looked around. A man was beside her bed staring at her. Hallie screamed, and the man hushed her. She noticed then that he was sitting cross-legged and hovering in midair to be at her eye level. She started screaming again.

"Quiet child, I'm not here to hurt you." The man hissed.

"The hell you're not, get out," Hallie screamed at him.

"If I wanted to hurt you, why would I ask you to wake?" he chided her.

Hallie swallowed back the scream thinking she was still dreaming "What do you want?"

To talk, that's all. It's a simple enough request for rational beings." Hallie nodded and realized she was sitting up. She scooted further back on the bed away from him. "You really are a beautiful woman,"

"Who are you?" Hallie asked.

"My name is Endali I'm a friend. I've come to show you where you belong." He explained.

"I don't understand. I belong here in New York."

He chuckled "This is your earthly home, I've come to show you, Underhill."

"Underhill? Why?"

"Because someone you love is of Underhill. You belong there with them. "

"And you know this person?"

"Quite well. Will you let me show you?" Endali asked.

"How do I know I can trust you?"

"Because I owe this person my life." He said seriously.

"Who?" He shook his head. He wasn't allowed to say. Hallie felt the stone around her neck heat and hoped beyond hope it was her father. She made a split second decision to go with him. "A quick trip, Liam will worry if I'm gone when he gets back."

"Aye, of course."

"Let me get dressed," She said climbing out of bed.

"I can help with that." He waved a hand, and her t-shirt and jogging pants were replaced by a purple silk off the shoulder dress. Her socks transformed into tan suede boots. "Oh but that hair." He complained. He waved a hand. Once again it behaved perfectly just as if Jenny wasted two hours curling and styling it into perfect waves.

"Thanks,"

Endali smiled slightly "Take my hand, and we'll be off." Hallie took his hand. "Now to get to Underhill is rather simple you've stumbled on it already. Close your eyes and remember, the sights as well as the smells. Then call to it with your heart."

"How... I don't understand."

"You escape there when you're scared." Hallie knew then, and she breathed as she gave in to the longing to be there. The smell of apple blossoms washed over her like an old friend. She the grass tickled her fingers. Birds sang as they flew on the warm breeze. All while Hallie stood amongst it and just breathed. When she opened her eyes, Hallie was immersed in sunlight. "Welcome to Underhill, Hallie."

"Can I see the one I love now?" Hallie asked.

"Rules forbid it. I'm sorry. But in time you will."

"What is this place?"

"Have a seat." He waved a hand, table, chairs and a full breakfast appeared. Hallie looked at the food worried as scenes from Alice in Wonderland ran through her head. "It won't bewitch you. I give my word." Hallie sat down and poured a glass of tea. "This is Underhill land of the Fae."

Hallie nearly choked "Fairies? You're a fairy, but aren't you supposed to fit in my pocket?"

"We can be as small or large as we want." Hallie was quiet then "We do not age as mortals do and do little else as mortals do."

"Wait, mortals? Does that mean..."

"Immortal for the most part. We can die, although mortals are hard pressed to achieve the task."

"So this is your home? And you what want me to stay here?" Hallie half laughed.

Endali shook his head. "Not me, the one you love."

Hallie stood up abruptly. "I can't just leave my life and everyone I care about. I'm engaged to be married. I want a life with Liam. I love..." Hallie sat back in her chair. She felt like the wind had been knocked out of her. She knew so little about Liam could it be him? No, it was impossible. She had to find out who wanted her here now. "How... how do I find out who wants me to stay here?"

Endali smiled. He was dazzling when he did. He had straight long brown hair, emerald eyes, and high cheekbones. When he smiled it lit up his whole face. If she didn't already know, he was something otherworldly Hallie would have guessed there was something different about him. That attention was focused on her now. It made her uncomfortable. "That is an excellent question." He leaned forward slightly. There will be a party, in two weeks. You are invited. You'll have to learn at least basic court protocol, but I can teach you that. And you can dance right?"

"Wait, court protocol?" Hallie asked confused.

"To meet the King and Queen." Endali shrugged it off. Hallie felt the air growing heavy, and the table began to tilt. Breathe she told herself. The King and Queen? Breathe, just breathe... of the fairies? No, she was going to faint. Endali caught her before she hit the ground. He smiled down at her and that only made matters worse. As everything faded to black Hallie felt a wave of warmth sweep over her. The panic faded, and she could breathe again. "So lessons should begin immediately. Can you find an excuse for me to be in the mortal realm with you?" Hallie stared at him dumbfounded. "Well you could stay here but its three months or more there." He shrugged.

"Come tomorrow afternoon with a suitcase you can be cousin Ed and stay with Jenny in my old room." Hallie sighed.

"Jenny? Is she as pretty as you?"

Hallie rolled her eyes. "Take me home."

Faolin

Faolin watched Hallie as she studied for her party. Kieran was playing his part well and following the rules for once. It killed him though to see her spend so much time with someone else. Every time Kieran moved too close or touched her for any reason Faolin wanted to tear him to pieces. He knew it bothered Hallie too, to lie to him. He was glad the this would all be over soon.

Two more mortal days, Faolin could hang on that long. Hallie made up some business trip. Cousin Ed was going to ask Jenny on a date before heading back to Iowa or where ever he was supposed to be visiting from. Liam said he'd go play soccer with his friends and catch up on his reading. Hallie still worried about him. He thought it was sweet.

As soon as Hallie was in Underhill though, Faolin followed. Taise greeted him in the field behind his home. The great white wolf was so happy to see him that he nearly knocked him over. Faolin missed his guardian as well. He ran his fingers through the thick fur enjoying the feel of it. Taise trotted beside him knowing the route to his room well. Faolin tried not to think of Hallie in Edali's home. Taise sensed his unease though and trotted off to the east. He'd go check on her then come back with details. Faolin smiled. There was a reason Taise was his guardian.

Faolin was drying off after his bath when he heard a knock. It was his aunt. He could sense her magic through the door. Faolin pulled on his underwear before telling her to enter. She smiled at him easily. He knew what she was thinking: this was a lot of trouble for a mortal. She didn't say it though. She never would. She handed him a glass of whiskey then his pants. Faolin took a drink before continuing to dress. His aunt tied his tie then kissed his cheek. "I'll be sure your uncle behaves." She slipped out without another word.

Straining his relationship with his aunt was his only regret about fighting with his uncle. If it weren't for her, he'd even enjoy it. The old mule had it coming half the time. If Faolin didn't challenge him no one would. He smiled and took another drink. All this for a mortal, he sighed. He loved her though. If this is what it took to get her, he'd do it a hundred times. Faolin pulled on his jacket and left his room. Taise stared up at him. Hallie was on her way.

Hallie

Hallie and Endali stood before the doors of the great hall. Her heart pounded as she waited for the doors to open. Finally, she heard a booming voice through the door, and it slowly swung open "Endali and his guest Hadleigh O'Neil." Hallie heard of his announcement, as Endali moved them forward. Hallie had no choice but to follow. People on either side began introducing themselves. She smiled politely and thanked them for their compliments. Hallie couldn't remember why she agreed to this now.

Endali saw something that made him drag Hallie closer to the front of the hall. Then she noticed it too, to the same man who'd announced them had made his way to the front of the room. "Good Fae Folk, give welcome to King Oberon and Queen Titania." Hallie bowed with everyone else in the room waiting for permission to rise.

Hallie could hear footsteps and then the hem of a silver dress. The king and queen stood before her. "You may rise my children" A loud but gentle voice urged. Hallie's heart jumped she thought she knew that voice. She rose slowly as her Endali began her introduction. "Sire may I present my guest, Hadleigh." Hallie looked up into the eyes of King Oberon. They were the same as Uncle Ron. Aunt Anya stood beside him. Liam stood slightly behind them with his arms folded lazily across his chest.

"Hello Hallie," he said in that familiar lilt. Hallie walked over and smacked him while half the court gasped and the other half laughed. Endali was laughing too. "How bout a dance then to cool you off."

Hallie wanted to protest, but she wanted answers more. She let him lead her onto the dance floor and waited for the music to start before speaking. "What the hell Liam? Is this some sort of game?"

He stopped turning for a moment "Never, I still want to marry you. I'll go tell the court now if you want."

"Why didn't you tell me you were Fae?"

"It was against the rules until you knew Underhill and met my Aunt and Uncle officially."

It almost hurt to look at Liam. He was so handsome in his tuxedo. Liam 's eyes sparkled like topazes. His blonde hair hung past his shoulders and was gathered in a neat ponytail at the base of his neck. Nothing made any sense. "Why me Liam? Look at the women here. I'm nothing compared to them."

He took her hand and led her outside. He sat down on a bench and waited for her to follow. “I saw you that first night you stumbled on Underhill. You weren't supposed to be able to do that. I came to the meadow that day ready to kill an intruder and found you instead. A beautiful mortal bathed in sunlight lost in the wonder of Underhill. I had to have you. I hadn't felt like that in centuries. I asked my King for the duty of tracking down the intruder and finding out how it was done.

“It took little effort to find you again. When I saw you though it was like the fog lifted. Suddenly I had a purpose again. I didn't know it Hallie, but I was falling in love with you. I haven't been in love in a very long time As much as I loved spending time with you Hallie, I fought it. A mortal caused my pain. I didn't want to go through it again. I couldn't stay away though and found excuses to stay. It annoyed my uncle to no end.

At my uncle's retreat, I fought with him. He was going to forbid me from pursuing marriage with you. It's you I want Hallie. In the end, he saw that and gave me leave to stay in the mortal realm. Everything since then has been for you.” He took her hand, and Hallie relented. The only thing I had to hide from you was my magic and true name, everything else was me. No one has ever let me be so free.”

“True name?” Hallie was confused.

“We'll get to that.” Liam smiled.

“And you really are King Oberon's nephew?” Hallie was still trying to grasp the concept.

“Here I only belong to Titania.” He saw the question in my eyes “History Hallie, too much history.”

“They both came to the mortal realm for you.” Hallie pointed out.

“He cares, but it doesn't stop his stubbornness. I will remain in his bad graces and therefore only my aunt's kin until I do something to please him.”

“Then why don't you?”

"Now why would I want to do that?" he grinned and Hallie knew there was something she was missing. "Am I forgiven?"

"I'm still mad. You have a lot of making up to do."

He took her hand and marched back inside to Endali stood chatting with the king and queen. "May I have the honor of a private dinner with Hadleigh tonight Endali?"

"Faolin this ball is in Hadleigh's honor tonight," Oberon warned.

"I asked her chaperone, Endali." Liam told the king. Hallie noticed Titania trying not to laugh.

"Hadleigh do you want to have dinner with Liam and miss meeting the people of Underhill?" Endali asked.

"There will be other opportunities for that." Hallie waved it off.

Endali looked at Oberon and nodded. "Go boy, but obey the rules." The king warned.

"Of course your highness." Liam snapped his fingers, and they appeared in a small dining room. A seating area was through a screen and closed doors most likely led to a bedroom. "My quarters." He smiled.

"I hope you're not expecting anything because I really am mad at you."

"I expected it." He waved a hand and a dinner as fine as any they ate in those fancy restaurants appeared. "Please have a seat."

Hallie sat down and ate a few bites of her chicken "What rules do you have to play by?"

"There's a whole list." Liam sighed. "They are tedious and make life very boring."

Hallie shook her head. "What sort of rules and why do you have to follow them?"

Liam set down his fork. "Rules meant to protect you." Hallie looked shocked. "I want to marry you, Hallie. But I can only stay in the mortal realm so long. Eventually, you're going to have to choose."

"What do you mean I have to choose?"

"You cannot constantly go back and forth. For one it risks exposure, but also as you age you will begin to lose your magic. So you must choose the mortal realm or Underhill."

"And what would you do if I chose to stay in the mortal realm?"

"I would have to leave you, Hallie." He saw the hurt in her eyes. "It wouldn't be fair to you. I wouldn't age, and I would have to cross back and forth regularly to maintain my magic."

"But it can be done."

"Oberon would not allow it."

"If I choose you I lose my mother. But how could I bear to lose you? Why would you ask me to marry you before you brought me here?""

"I had to. You had to be committed before we revealed our secrets." Hallie looked like she was going to cry. "I'm sorry Hallie if there was another way I would have taken it.

They finished dinner saying little else. Hallie had a thousand questions but was beginning to fear the answers. She also wasn't sure what to think of Liam. She still loved him no matter what he was, but he'd lied. The fact that he had good reason didn't change the facts. She went home after dinner only letting Liam kiss her cheek. She probably should have gone back to the ball, but she didn't want to speak to anyone.

Faolin

Faolin cursed as soon as Hallie left his presence. He was going to lose her if he wasn't vigilant. Liam had been so careful to follow the rules. Now it may cost him everything. Hallie wasn't Fae, she wasn't like some of the other mortal women he'd encountered either. She had a sense of honor that she lived by. Hallie thought everyone else should live by that some code. Liam lied to her, and it went against everything she believed. Liam tried to explain it to her, but he'd blundered it.

There had to be a way to make Hallie see he did everything for her. That the only reason he lied was to allow their marriage in the first place. She didn't understand Fae life or its rules. Faolin let out a frustrated grunt. Taise pushed his head under Faolin's hand then his back. Faolin let his fingers run through the thick white fur. Taise's presence always calmed him. The wolf looked up at him a moment before trotting off.

Faolin tried to sleep that night. There was little use. Not only was he worried about what lay ahead, but he'd also grown accustomed to Hallie next to him. Faolin got out of bed and paced. Usually, he was a patient hunter when it came to Hallie though Faolin couldn't stand the uncertainty. There was only one way to fix this. Faolin formed a portal and stepped through to Hallie's room.

Taise was already there sleeping at the foot of her bed. The wolf looked up at Faolin's entrance. His tail wagged slightly before he laid his head back down on his paws. Faolin sat on the edge of Hallie's bed. She slept soundly, and Faolin longed to crawl into bed beside her. Instead, he woke her gently.

Hallie sat up disoriented. Her eyes scanned the room. When she saw Taise, she backed up as far as she could until she hit the headboard. It wasn't until she heard Faolin's voice that she calmed down. "Taise is my guardian, he came to watch you. He would never hurt you." Faolin told her.

"He's huge Liam," Hallie said unsurely."

Taise raised his head to study her then lowered it again looking bored. "Taise, leave us for now." The wolf got up stretching as he went. He walked through the closed door leaving them alone. Hallie was white. Faolin threw his arms around her. "I'm so sorry, Hallie. I forgot you aren't used to all this."

"I'm fine Liam,"

"I never wanted to lie to you. If it weren't for my vow, I never would have. I wanted to tell you everything so many times." Faolin told her as he held her close.

Hallie kissed him gently then snuggle into his arms. "I understand Liam,"

"Does this mean I'm forgiven?"

"I was more hurt than anything. I still am a little, but I love you, Liam." He kissed her neck as she spoke making it hard to concentrate.

"Faolin," He corrected.

She looked up at him confused. "What?"

"All Fae have true names. It holds power over them and are closely guarded. My true name is Faolin. You are one of three people other than me to know it." He explained.

"Why would you tell me Li... Faolin?"

"I love you, I want you beside me for the rest of my life. I trust you with everything Hallie."

"You really mean it don't you?" Hallie smiled and kissed him.

He stopped kissing her and looked downright serious. It worried Hallie. "There is something else Hallie. Something about my past that you should know before you decide to put me in your good graces." Hallie stared unable to say anything. "Underhill used to be part of the mortal realm. We lived in peace with the mortals, some thought of us as demigods even and left tokens so we would bless their homes and families. But soon the old beliefs began to die, and Underhill lost its footing in that realm as the mortals lost belief. Oberon found a new way to anchor Underhill j truly making him the Forest Lord. We lived in peace until the mortals saw us as heathen gods and rebelled cutting down our forests.

"It started a war. Oberon would not allow mortals to banish him from this realm. My father was married to Titania's sister and fought beside both Oberon and Titania." Faolin saw her flinch. "Her hands are not clean. She killed many men in her day. When I was six, my father was killed. It is a hard thing to do, to kill a Fairy but he was surrounded and butchered. When my mother heard the news, she took her own life, and I was left an orphan.

"Oberon raised me as his own son teaching me the ways of war as well as the duty of leadership. When I was 16, I rode into battle beside him exactly where my father once stood. Many mortals lost their lives at my hands. I was so proficient Oberon gave me my own men. We used to hunt from the woods killing at all hours of the night. Then we would strike again in the morning. Anything to set them off balance. It was the mortals that named me Faolin.

"After 15 years of slaughter, they figured out our weakness and began attacking the trees again. Without our foothold here we could not attack so easily. Eventually, only a few trees survived. The war was over. My services were rewarded I was named Prince Faolin, Oberon's only heir. I was given quarters and anything else I wanted.

"Those in Underhill wanted to start a new era. One that forgot about the mortals altogether. Oberon made a push for couples to have children and tried to do the same with Titania. But few had luck, and the Queen herself was left wanting. Oberon slipped the borders and brought a mortal woman back and gave her to one of his lords nine months later there was a new child in Underhill.

"Breeding with mortals became common practice after that and stolen women commonplace. I watched it all with disdain. I was taught my whole life that they were like animals not worthy of us. To lower ourselves by breeding with them was distasteful to me. My uncle said nothing of my attitude as long as I kept it to myself.

"I rarely came to court preferring the solitude of the hills and the thrill of the hunt. But one day I happened to be there when a new mortal was brought in. Ianthe was the most beautiful woman I'd ever seen. There was a spirit in her too, wild and fierce. I asked my uncle for her immediately, but he refused. My own past finally caught up to me, and he assumed I meant to hurt her. She was given to Lokesh. Before I could convince my uncle and stop Lokesh, he had already taken her and Ianthe was with child.

"It sent me over the edge. I stole Ianthe from Lokesh hiding her in the mortal realm. I told my uncle I killed her because she had betrayed me with Lokesh. Oberon's justice was swift. I was stripped of my title and from then on only Titania's nephew. My quarters were moved to the far reaches of the castle and barley rivaled a guest suite.

"I never cared, Ianthe gave birth to a healthy boy. Then almost two years later I had a son. She was happy with me and the life I provided. I loved both boys, but I hate to admit that I let my son beat on Lokesh's more than I should have. They both turned out to be fine men though and married.

"Lokesh discovered my secret and found Ianthe and both our sons while I was in Underhill He killed all five of them. Ianthe, my son, his wife, even his own son, and wife. Only my granddaughter remained. Lokesh had missed her. As much as I loved that little girl I had no stomach to raise her. I took her to a poor family in town and paid them to raise her as their own. Then I returned to Underhill and took Lokesh's life."

"Shit, what did Oberon do?"

"What could he do? Lokesh killed my family."

"You killed soldiers and innocent mortals didn't you." He nodded. "What does Faolin mean?"

"Wolf," Hallie looked to the door. "Taise has been by my side for most of my life. He is my guardian and my friend."

"He fought by your side didn't he?" Faolin nodded. " You're not that Fairy anymore." He shook his head. "Your Halloween costume really was part of your history then."

"I wore something similar during the happier part with Ianthe and my sons."

"You didn't ride to battle in that." He shook his head. "Can I see?" he flinched.

"Hallie I don't think it's a good idea."

"It's part of you. I won't leave I promise." Faolin stood before her, and his clothes changed. His pants changed to a green plaid. His shirt disappeared, and his chest was covered with blue swirls of paint that continued up his neck and face. His hair was pulled partially up and braided, but the rest was wild. A sword hung at one hip and an ax on the other, he wore no shoes. He was frightening, yet strangely Hallie found him absolutely gorgeous. He looked worried until Hallie spoke, "Somehow it fits you."

He gave a disgusted growl and the clothes he wore earlier reappeared. "You wouldn't think so if you saw me then."

"I know you now Faolin that's all that matters." She pulled him down beside her wrapping her arms around him. "The paint was kind of sexy."

"It was meant to scare mortals."

"I love a Fae remember." Faolin let out a heavy breath. Hallie unbuttoned his shirt, and he didn't stop her. "You could keep part of it as a tattoo, here" she ran her finger around his chest and upper arm.

"Crazy girl," he growled as he grabbed her and pinned her beneath him. Hallie giggled as he kissed her neck.

"Oh just try it out."

"Maybe I need some incentive." Hallie kissed him running her nails down his back. He pulled her tighter against him. It was only after Hallie saw part of the pattern recreated in black on his shoulder and chest that she gave into her desire.

Hallie

Hallie noticed Faolin admire the tattoo as he pulled his shirt on. She was glad he liked it because she wasn't going to let him get rid of it just like she wasn't going to let him cut his hair. She knew exactly who he was now and she wanted all of him. The realization scared Hallie. Staying here meant she had to give up everything in the mortal realm. Before she did that there were a few things to finish there and a few questions left for Faolin.

"Why can't I be like your other wives Faolin and stay in the mortal realm?" Hallie asked.

"I've never married before. I thought about it with Ianthe something wasn't right though. I never had the urge to tell her anything, she knew part of my past and Underhill because of Lokesh, but I never told her my true name. You are different. I wanted to tell you everything from the beginning. Marriage is an important decision for us. It is permanent, and forever is a very long time in Underhill. Once married if anything happened to you I would be lost like my mother. If we stayed in the mortal realm Hallie, you would grow old before my eyes and die. I can't think of worse torture."

"And if I stay I won't age?" he shook his head. "And you won't lose interest."

"Never,"

"How old are you Faolin?"

He thought a long moment and Hallie took that as a bad sign "I don't know between 1,000 and 1,100 mortal years. We don't really keep track."

"How many children have you brought to Underhill?" Hallie asked.

"None, oh I have had a dozen. They were mine, not the Fae's. I would not share them."

"The reason why you and Oberon still aren't at peace?" Hallie guessed.

"In part, but mostly we are too much alike." He grinned.

Hallie was sure she must be crazy. If she agreed to marry Faolin and live in Underhill, she would give up everything and everyone else she ever loved. He was perfect though, and he loved her. Faolin loved everything about her. Where else would she find that? Hallie kissed Faolin "I love you, I always will. It doesn't matter what you are or where we live."

Faolin took Halie in his arms. He held her tight and Hallie felt the heat radiating off Faolin. His lips brushed hers, and she was instantly on fire. He laid her back in bed and before she realized it they were making love again.

Hallie woke the next morning in Faolin's arms. The sun streamed through her window making her whole room bright and cheery. There was a knock on the door. Hallie pulled the covers up hoping they would go away. It didn't work. The door creaked open a few seconds later.

Endali came in, "Your Uncle is going to be pissed if he finds out about this," he laughed.

Faolin sat up a little, "Who's going to tell him?" he raised a brow.

"Alright Liam," Endali waved him off.

"We are telling Oberon to make it official today." Faolin kissed Hallie as Endali left.

Chapter 7

H*allie*

A week passed in the mortal world while they were in Underhill. Hallie was glad she arranged the time off at work. As soon as she got back, she called her mom. She was happy to hear from Hallie. He mom was the main reason Hallie returned. She wanted to spend some time with her before Hallie left the mortal realm forever.

During the week Hallie's work kept her extremely busy, weekends were spent in New Jersey with her mom. After two months Hallie was utterly exhausted. She couldn't believe it had been nearly three weeks since they'd spent an evening together. All she wanted was a quiet dinner and a night of lovemaking.

Hallie opened the door to their apartment and was horrified. Alainya was in Faolin's arms with her legs wrapped around him. His slacks were on the floor, and her skirt was hitched up. Faolin was already pushing her away, but Hallie had seen enough. She stormed out the door. Faolin rushed after her grabbing at his pants, but they fell down around his ankles tripping him. Hallie heard him run down the hall after her as the elevator doors closed. The man in the elevator beside her said nothing as she wiped tears away, but he certainly jumped when Faolin appeared in the elevator.

"Damn it, Liam," Hallie swore. He waved a hand, making the man ignore them completely.

"That wasn't what it looked like," Faolin said in his defense.

"Oh really, it was pretty obvious to me."

"Hallie please,"

"With all the people it had to be her." Hallie spat "And to think I thought you disliked her. You really had me convinced."

"I do Hallie, please you must believe me."

"Yet you sleep with her."

"No, I didn't."

"Then what was that?"

"She wanted you to think..."

"Oh, of course, it was Alainya's elaborate scheme...Ughh how could I be so stupid? You were probably diddling her on the cruise too, that's why I always saw her leaving when I was coming."

"No, Hallie I swear." The elevator stopped, and the man got off. "I caught you in the act Faolin."

He looked away "She only wants you to think..."

"Why would she care?" Hallie pulled off her ring and handed it to him. "Here I don't want this. Go home Faolin." Hallie jumped when he disappeared. Then she remembered Faolin told her a Fae's true name held power over them. Hallie sighed hopefully that meant he'd stay in Underhill.

Hallie went to her old apartment. Liam cut her a break on the rent because Hallie moved in with him. Luckily it made Jenny lazy about finding a new roommate. Hallie laid on the couch and cried until she was numb. Jenny came home a short while later and was ready to kick in Liam's teeth for what he'd done. She went to the store for some chunky monkey and found Hallie exactly where she'd left her when she returned. Jenny urged Hallie up and placed a spoon in her hand.

Hallie didn't go to work the next day, too depressed to move. Breakfast was the leftover ice cream from the night before. Halfway through the pint, her phone rang. Hallie hadn't even realized she'd turned it back on. Faolin called six times in an hour the night before, and she'd turned it off. The number on caller ID surprised her now. It was Sharon there was an emergency at work. Hallie could avoid her personal life if she threw herself into work.

Faolin

Faolin did everything he could think of to win Hallie back. At first, he tried calling and texting her. Eventually, she blocked his number. Faolin went to Jenny and tried to explain. Her roommate could have been mistaken for Fae with her temperament. The woman threatened to do unspeakable things to his manhood. Faolin went to her job. He faked a modeling job trying to get in, but Sharon had him banned from the building.

Then Faolin started sending cards, flowers, and gifts. Most of them were returned. He couldn't understand why Hallie wouldn't even give him the chance to explain. He watched her many nights without her ever knowing. Faolin couldn't help it, he was worried about her.

Hallie avoided him in the building as well, even though Faolin went out of his way to see her every day. She regularly altered her routine by either leaving at a different time or taking a different route to the front doors. Faolin had to resort to magic to see her. It only made Hallie angrier in the end, and he stopped doing so.

Three months without Hallie though was taking its toll. He needed to find a way to get her back. It was all he could think about. He had one option left, although he hadn't wanted to use it. At this point though Faolin was desperate. He waited until late that evening and lay in his bed.

Hallie

Hallie heard someone call her name. She looked around. She was all alone. Then Hallie felt the urge to move. Why the hell did she feel compelled to move? She glanced at the clock. It was midnight. Hallie went to bed at 11 o'clock, maybe this was a dream. Hallie heard the sounds from the street and the drip from the bathroom faucet. No probably not, she never noticed those in dreams. Hallie heard it again and felt the compulsion to move. To go where though? Hallie focused on the destination. Faolin's apartment.

Oh no. Hallie refused. "Faolin, nephew of Titania and Oberon Queen and King of the Fae I order you to stop bothering me." Everything stopped. Whatever Hallie did must have worked. She rolled over to sleep and started to cry instead.

The following Monday Hallie got a call she never expected. "Ms. O'Neil, this is Mr. Barrows, I own the management company for your building which means I'm Liam's boss."

"Yes Mr. Barrows, how can I help you?" Hallie responded confused.

"Liam hasn't been answering his calls this afternoon. I was wondering if you'd seen him."

"I haven't seen him in three months."

"He said you'd broken up, but I was still hoping you might..."

"No Mr. Barrows, have you tried his apartment?"

"I'm not in the city but, I called his personal cell no one answered. He was ill last week, and I'm a little worried."

"Ill?" Hallie was beginning to worry too Fae didn't get ill.

"Yes ill,"

"I have a key, I'll check on him."

"Thank you, Ms. O'Neil."

Hallie hung up the phone "Damn you Faolin get your ass here right this moment." Nothing happened. He'd waited all this time to ignore her now; the thought made Hallie mad. She went upstairs to Faolin's apartment and let herself in. He was lying in bed wracked with sweat even though his skin was ice. He saw Hallie "I didn't do it, Hallie, she used magic, she wants you to think... she doesn't want us to marry... she wants me dead... she..."

He rambled on, but Hallie stopped him "Dead?"

"Magic's almost gone." He managed a smile for her.

"Go home Faolin," Hallie said frustrated.

"Can't" he swallowed.

"And why not?" he looked up at her holding out her engagement ring.

Hallie gasped "Because I broke it off?" he nodded. "You can't go back without me?" he nodded again; his eyes fighting to stay open. "You risked everything for me, but why?"

He smiled weakly "I love you," it was barely a whisper, but Hallie heard it she took the engagement ring from him and slipped it on.

"Faolin I'm so sorry." She kissed his brow before pulling his arm around her shoulder and hauling him up. She called to Underhill, and it appeared before her with its familiar scent. As soon as she stepped through, she shouted for Taise. The wolf appeared out of nowhere making her jump. Taise waited as Hallie laid Faolin on his back. Then he opened a portal for both of them to Faolin's room. It surprised Hallie that Taise could use magic to get Faolin into bed.

Oberon barged through the doors just Hallie pulled the covers up. "What a mess," he commented then looked at her "you waited long enough."

"If Alainya wouldn't have interfered he wouldn't be in this state."

"Alainya?"

"She tried to convince me they were having an affair and I believed it."

"He hates Alainya," he said confused.

"She was very convincing." Hallie sighed looking to Faolin "Will he be alright?"

"He'll be good as new in a few days." Faolin was already breathing easier, and his skin was warmer. "You choose to go back, and he goes with you."

Hallie nodded "I will stay, but I have to tell my mother where I went or she'll be worried sick."

"I wouldn't advise leaving for a while" Oberon meant even if she left for a short time Faolin would have to go as well. "It's the law until you're married."

"I will obey, but I need to call her."

"You have a phone," Oberon snorted and left.

Faolin

Faolin woke hours later to Hallie stroking his hair. He tried to apologize to Hallie. She told him there wasn't any need. She said she believed him now. Faolin was delirious with a fever and broke the rules. He told her how he wasn't allowed to return to Underhill without her until they were married. He also confessed that he was near death because his magic was nearly gone. Faolin was sure his uncle was going to murder him. Hallie said he already knew though. He hadn't said one word about it.

Faolin breathed a sigh of relief. He had Hallie back, and he didn't have to worry about his uncle's wrath. In a couple days they could return to the mortal realm and tie up loose ends before starting their life in Underhill.

Over the next couple days, Hallie finally seemed content in Faolin's presence. She no longer second-guessed his choice. Hallie quit looking at the Fae women with suspicion. It was as if Faolin's brush with death made her realize just how much he loved her. Faolin thought it silly, but if that's what it took, he wasn't going to argue.

Hallie said this time they would return for six months. She was going to tell her mom they were moving to the UK. After the wedding, Hallie was going to slowly distance herself from her mother over a few years. Eventually, she would have to cut all ties, she had a little time though. What were a few years in the millennia they had to look forward to?

Before they returned to the mortal realm, Faolin had to speak with Oberon. As the king, he reminded Faolin that he was still bound by the rules of his engagement to Hallie. He made Faolin repeat them for good measure. Then he told him that Alainya had not returned to Underhill yet. When she did though, it was up to the court to decide her punishment. Faolin understood no matter what Oberon claimed they were still family and he had to remain impartial.

As his uncle, Oberon told him to be careful. He was worried that Alainya might try something else. Faolin was already preparing defenses against her. The best way to hurt him now was through Hallie, and he wasn't going to let that happen.

Hallie

Life went back to normal in their tiny apartment. Faolin made up an excuse about a family emergency with his boss, Mr. Barrows. The man was very nice and accepted the explanation. Hallie Told Sharon the same thing. She got to keep her job, although Hallie was out of PTO. Her pay was docked for a week. Sharon was more worried that Hallie was back together with Liam. She told Hallie that she was making a mistake. She'd already heard the same concerns from Jenny. It was Hallie's mistake to make. If anything happened, she had to live with the consequences. Sharon told her to be careful and to come to work on Monday.

Hallie slowed things down a little at work. Sharon was disappointed. What was the point though of rushing around like crazy for a career she was going to quit in less than a year? Their last month in the mortal realm, Hallie was going to stay in New Jersey with her mom. They were also going to have a small ceremony for her. The actual wedding though would be in Underhill.

Faolin insisted on some sort of spell even though his aunt specifically told Hallie not to let him use his magic. Whatever he did was supposed to protect them from Alainya. If it kept that bitch out of her fiancé's pants, she'd let Faolin cast a spell or two.

Ten weeks after returning to the mortal realm Hallie returned from a long day of work. She called out for Faolin like she normally did as opened the door. There was no answer. She checked her phone. Normally if he had to go on a call, he sent her a text, nothing. Hallie set her purse down and went into their apartment. Normally she'd grab a weapon but if Faolin wasn't responding they weren't dealing with a normal intruder.

A few steps in she saw the mess in the living room. Books were everywhere, the couch looked like it exploded, the coffee table was in splinters, and there were scorch marks on the ceiling. What the hell happened? "Faolin I summon thee." Hallie saw a glimmer of light appear then fade. "Faolin nephew of Queen Titania and King Oberon, I summon thee." The light appeared again and faded. Something was wrong. He heard the summons and was trying to respond.

Hallie had no magic of her own. She couldn't go to Faolin. Maybe he could bring Hallie to him though. "Faolin bring Hadleigh Aoife O'Neil to you." The light flared for the third time more strongly. It lasted longer, but it faded too. Hallie cursed. She had no idea what to do now. She needed help. Hallie closed her eyes and called to Underhill. Going there now was as easy as breathing. Hallie stepped through the portal and ran for help.

Faolin

The room Faolin was being held in was like any other. There was a bed and a window. It was late out now, and the moon was full. Trying to answer Hallie's summons was a dumb thing to do. Faolin wasted a lot of magic. It was something he couldn't afford to do. His captors knew that too. They were counting on it. Faolin had no clue how he was going to get out of this though.

All of Faolin's protective efforts were focused on Hallie. He never thought they would come after him directly. Faolin was overconfident. Now it could cost him everything. He ran his hand over the protective shield and watched it ripple. It took two Fae's magic to contain him. If he had all his magic, it wouldn't matter. He was Titania's nephew, and King Oberon didn't settle when he chose his bride.

The door opened. The shield parted just enough for Alainya to step through. Her movements were always liquid silk, and it gave Faolin the chills. "How the mighty have fallen Lord Liam." She mocked.

"Alainya, there will be a price to pay for this," Faolin warned.

"I don't really care. First I kill you, then that mortal you've grown attached to, and finally, I'll skin that wolf of yours alive." She smiled.

"Taise is a guardian, he's protected by Fae law," Faolin growled.

"He threw his lot in with you when he helped you murder Lokesh." She snarled.

"Lokesh butchered my whole family. He was so blinded by rage he killed his own son and daughter in law. I was within my rights when I took his life."

"I'm not having this argument again." She turned her back on Faolin, "I loved Lokesh, we were getting married, and you murdered him over a few mortals. It's time you pay Liam."

Hallie

Hallie was looking for Endali. She found King Oberon instead. When Hallie tried to tell him what happened, she started crying. It was the sheer frustration of not knowing what happened. Oberon was kind though. Kinder than Hallie ever guessed he would be. He wrapped his arms around Hallie and coaxed the information out of her.

When Hallie finished, she had no clue what to do. She felt better though. "What do I do now? I have no magic. How can a mortal defeat a Fae?"

"Two, and you can't," He told her. Hallie was ready to cry again. "Faolin could if he had all of his magic and wasn't worried about using it."

Tell me how." Hallie said.

"A bargain then," Oberon suggested.

Hallie wasn't sure. She heard stories about the Forest Lord's treachery when it came to deals. "What are the terms?

"I tell you how to save Faolin, and you provide me with an heir." Hallie looked at the king with suspicion.

"What's the catch?" Hallie asked.

"This is as wide open of a bargain as I ever give." He offered.

"I need the information to free him from the two Fae who are holding him at this time." Hallie clarified. "And I don't want to have your child I want to have Faoilin's."

"Agreed," He offered his hand.

"Faolin and I raise our children not you," Hallie added.

Oberon laughed and shook her hand. "When I offer an open deal it isn't specific to help you. But good for you Hallie. Wait till I tell Titania." He shook his head. "Faolin can save himself. He only needs his magic, to restore it. You must free him from his vows."

"We have to marry to do that," Hallie reasoned.

"You know his true name," Oberon shrugged. "Swear to be his. Then you can go to him."

Hallie took a deep breath, "Faolin nephew of Queen Titania and King Oberon I Hadleigh Aoife O'Neil swear to love you for all time, to be with you and only you, you are mine Faolin, and I am yours." The air swirled around Hallie, She felt it crackle. Every fiber of her being seemed to sizzle a moment with white heat. For a fleeting moment, she felt Faolin. He was elated then saddened. The connection faded, She was alone.

Hallie looked at Oberon he smiled slightly. "Go bring him home then we can talk about an heir."

Faolin

Alainya backed Faolin into a corner. No matter what he did, this wasn't going to be pleasant. He could fight her with magic until it was gone then die of sickness. Or He could fight Alainya off physically. Eventually, she would overpower him with her magic there too. Faolin had to try though. He owed it to Hallie. He had a better shot with his brute strength if he could catch her before she could use her magic.

The room was laced with traps though. It made Faolin weak physically too. As soon as he moved against Alainya, he felt weak and tired. She must have planned for this since her first attempt failed. Alainya came towards him with a dagger in hand. Then he heard his name. Hallie was speaking. She pledged her love and devotion... forever. Faolin felt his magic return. Alainya didn't know though. How could she?

Hallie appeared directly in front of Faolin. Alainya seized the unexpected opportunity and lunged forward plunging the blade into Hallie. She screamed in pain as the dagger hit bone. Hallie tried to push Alainya off. The Fae woman held on tight. Faolin was beyond angry with Alainya. Another member of his family was being attacked. With his magic returned Alainya's magic had little effect on him. He stepped around Hallie and grabbed Alainya's head. Faolin gave a quick jerk, and her neck snapped. Alainya's body fell to the floor with a heavy thud.

Faolin's first instinct was to help Hallie but Alainya's idiot cousin, Tanner was still there somewhere. He wasn't very bright and always did what she said. Faolin summoned Taise to guard Hallie while he searched for Tanner.

The apartment they were in wasn't very big. Tanner sat in front of a tv in the living room. He was eating cereal out of the box. Faolin could have used a spell to knock him out, but right now brute force was much more satisfying. He sent the unconscious Tanner and Alainya's body back to his uncle not caring what the consequences were.

Luckily Hallie's wound wasn't as bad as he thought it was. Alainya hit a rib going in which made her miss Hallie's heart and anything else important. The blade was deep though. The tip hit her scapula on the other side. Despite easing the pain with magic, Hallie passed out when Faolin pulled the dagger free.

Taise laid down beside her keeping Hallie warm. In the middle of the healing, she came to again. Hallie was so happy to see him that she started crying. He wanted to yell at her for putting herself in danger. Right then he couldn't muster the energy. He was just relieved she was safe, and they were together again.

That night Faolin took Hallie back to his rooms in Underhill. He swore his vows to her making everything official. Faolin was sure

Titania would insist on a formal wedding. The Fae loved an excuse to throw a party. That evening though everything else was forgotten. It was only them.

Hallie

Hallie lay in bed with Faolin perfectly content. They'd spent half the night making love. Faolin never seemed to tire of her. If she spent the rest of her life like this, she would die happy. He kissed her cheek. Hallie just fell asleep when there was a knock on the door. Faolin got up annoyed. He said it was his uncle.

As soon as Faolin opened the door, King Oberon strode into their room. "There's the happy couple." He smiled. "Better get dressed, busy day today. The whole kingdom is assembling now so you might as well put on your tux."

Hallie sat up pulling the covers around her. "Why are they assembling?"

"This is big news Hallie," King Oberon pat his nephew on the back. There was a knock on the door. Oberon waved them in. A servant carried in dresses. "My queen sent dresses for you to borrow and some jewelry Hallie. I'll see you both in an hour." The servant sat down his burden and left with the king.

Hallie picked up a purple nearly backless dress. "You'll look stunning in it. Although the red will make your skin look radiant." He kissed her shoulder. Hallie smiled at Faolin. The most gorgeous man she ever saw said such things to her. Now he was hers. They would be married for countless years. Hallie couldn't help smiling.

"Get dressed," Faolin chided.

Hallie stood outside the doors to the main hall with Faolin. He looked through as they swung open. He shook his head. "He wasn't kidding. The whole kingdom is here." He thought out loud.

"Hallie, what gave you the idea to marry me at that moment?" he asked

"Your Uncle," Hallie confessed. When Faolin looked concerned she continued. "We made a deal, but I was sure to be specific."

"Hallie, you never make deals with the Fae. Especially not Oberon."

"Do you want to know the deal or not?" Faolin nodded. Hallie explained everything and waited.

Faolin rubbed his hands on his face. "Woman, what have you done?" Hallie was confused. He groaned. "I should have seen this coming. He's naming me the heir. I can't get out of it. You swore I would."

"No, I didn't... I just... but," Hallie stammered.

There wasn't time to explain anything. Faolin's aunt arrived a moment later. She smiled kindly at him. Then she pulled him into a hug. "Think what you will Faolin, but you have always been my son. His too. We can't be happier for you. This is where you belong." Titania let him go and turned to Hallie. She smiled. "Yes, I see it now." Oberon passed by all of them without a word taking his queen's hand, leading her in.

That evening Hallie stood with Faolin on the balcony of their new rooms. She couldn't believe how big they were. They could fit a small house in those rooms. Everything was so beautiful too. Faolin assured her they could change anything she required. Hallie didn't really care though. She had everything she wanted. Faolin was more than enough.

Faolin held her close as they watched the sunset. He kissed her cheek. Tomorrow was a new day. Titania started Hallie's lessons on court laws. There was a wedding to plan and endless dress fittings. All Hallie desired now was a night alone with her prince. She took Faolin by the hand and led him inside.

Also by Rebecca Tran

Box Set
Dragons of the North

Chronicles of the Coranydas
A Guardian Falls
The Rashade'

Dragons of the South
Hunted
Sweet Surrender
Primal Instincts

Standalone
Neutral Space
Magic Always Has a Price
Honor Bound
For Their Sins

Watch for more at rtranbook.net.

About the Author

Rebecca Tran is an award-winning author, reviewer and blogger. She started writing when she was sixteen as self-prescribed therapy after her father passed away and hasn't stopped since. Rebecca is also a pharmacist, and mother to two rambunctious girls and a Boston Terrier and Pitt Bull. If she ever has free time she likes combing resale shops to add to her teapot collection or quilting. Currently, she lives in her home state of Missouri.

Read more at rtranbook.net.

www.ingramcontent.com/pod-product-compliance
Lightning Source LLC
LaVergne TN
LVHW091122150826
845673LV00002B/942

* 9 7 9 8 2 3 0 4 0 1 0 3 2 *